With Love From BOOKY

Bernice Thurman Hunter

Cover photograph by Kathryn Cole

Scholastic-TAB Publications Ltd.
123 Newkirk Road, Richmond Hill, Ontario, Canada

The author acknowledges use of "Be good, sweet maid" from "A Farewell" by
Charles Kingsley.

Grateful acknowledgment is made to the author for the photographs on pages 1, 137 and 141; to
the Eaton's Archives for the photographs on pages 12 and 61; to the *Globe and Mail* for
permission to reprint the article from the July 15, 1936 *Globe* on page 125.

Canadian Cataloguing in Publication Data

Hunter, Bernice Thurman.
    With love from Booky

ISBN 0-590-71220-9

I. Title.

PS8565.U57W47   jC813'.54   C83-098639-1
PZ7.H86Wi

3rd printing 1988   **Printed in Canada by Webcom Limited**

With love to my grandchildren,
Meredith, Lisa, Hunter and Franceline

Contents

1
Cousins and 'lations

The summer I was sent away to Muskoka was the summer of my first big crush. I was madly in love with Georgie Dunn. He was one of the few kids in our gang who wasn't my cousin, so it was all right to be in love with him.

Almost everybody on Veeny Street was related in one way or another. For instance, my friend Gladie's father was my grandfather's brother. I thought this was sort of strange because Gladie and I were the same age. Ruthie's mother, who lived in the house next door, was my mother's first cousin. And Ada-May, who lived up the street, was Ruthie's second cousin on her mother's side and my third cousin on her father's side and I think she was Gladie's fourth cousin but I'm not sure what side.

Then there was Uncle Andy, who lived all by himself at the corner of Veeny and Mayberry in an old frame house with no electricity or bathroom. He was my great-uncle by marriage, but Great-Aunt Veeny, the one our street was named after, had got galloping consumption and gone home—that's what

Mum called heaven—just three months after their wedding day.

All these cousins and 'lations—that's how Grampa Cole pronounced relations—were on Mum's side. Dad's family still lived in the log house his grandfather had built in Muskoka about a hundred years ago. Except for Uncle Charlie's family, who lived on Gerrard Street in Toronto. He had a barbershop in his front room instead of regular furniture, and he gave us free haircuts.

There were literally hundreds of us cousins and 'lations in Swansea, all descended from the very first settlers to emigrate from Swansea in Wales. That's how our little village on the western outskirts of Toronto got its name.

It was swell belonging to such a big, boisterous clan. But there was one drawback to being blood relations that all us kids had been warned about, and that was, when we grew up we could never marry each other or we'd all have crazy children like Roy-Roy the dumb boy.

Roy-Roy wore a flannelette bib around his neck and he slobbered and jabbered like a baby even though he was fourteen years old, the same age as Georgie and my brother Arthur. Roy-Roy and his mother, Raggie-Rachel, lived in a tar-paper shack down by Catfish Pond. Roy-Roy caught catfish with his bare hands—I even saw him do it once! Raggie-Rachel picked the dump for a living. We nicknamed her Raggie-Rachel because she always wore about five raggedy dresses piled on top of each other. Nobody knew who Roy-Roy's father was, but the grownups whispered behind their hands that he must have been Rachel's blood relation or how else could you account for Roy-Roy? Anyway, Mum said they were no kith or kin of ours.

So even though our gang was roughly made up of half boys and half girls, our friendships were mostly 'plutonic.' At least that's what my big sister Willa said, and she ought to know because she had just graduated into Fifth Form high school at the top of her class and she knew just about everything.

It was the end of June, 1935, and I had passed, by the skin of my teeth, into Senior Fourth. I was gleefully looking forward to hundreds of hot summer days, free as a bird, running all over Swansea, swimming in Lake Ontario, going to Sunnyside Amusement Park, playing street games and roasting swiped potatoes down in the woodsy hollows of the Camel's Back, when I suddenly took sick.

My chest went all wheezy and my face turned as grey as the sidewalk. At first Mum tried doctoring me herself; then, when that didn't work, she asked Maude Sundy to come over and take a look at me. Maude was our landlady but she was also a registered nurse, so everybody in Swansea called on her when they got sick. Well Maude rubbed my chest with hot camphorated oil and dosed me with Friar's Balsam and purged me with Epsom salts and said I had to eat lots of eggs.

So Dad went right out and bought half a dozen eggs just for me, and Mum fixed me a lovely poached egg on toast every day. But when a week went by and I didn't show any signs of improve-

ment, Maude said Mum had better take me to see a
real doctor on Bloor Street.

Her name was Doctor Smelley—no kidding—and
she was really nice so I decided I'd be a doctor when
I grew up if doctors didn't have to be good in arithmetic. Well, Dr. Smelley said I had a bad case of
bronchitis and it might turn into TB at any minute
and what I needed in the worst way was fresh air
and sunshine.

"You'll have to go to your Aunt Aggie's in Muskoka, Booky," Mum said, rubbing her hands together in that agitated way she had when she was
worried. ("Boo-key" was the nickname she'd given
me when I was a little kid.)

"But there's lots of fresh air and sunshine right
here in Swansea, Mum!" I protested wheezily.

"Oh, pshaw, Bea." Mum's dark eyes were bright
with fear. "What about all that black smoke belch-
ing out of the Bolt Works? And those awful fumes
coming off the dump not a stone's throw from our
front stoop? Why, it's enough to sicken a pig. No,
Bea, I'm scared for you. You'll have to go to Muskoka."

Of course, I knew what she was scared of, that I'd
get consumption and go galloping home in less than
twenty-four hours, just like Great-Aunt Veeny did. I
also knew that her decision was for my own good,
but I could hardly stand the thought of being away
for the whole summer and missing all the fun on
Veeny Street.

And there was another reason why I didn't want
to go. I hadn't breathed it to a living soul, not even

4

to Gladie, who was my best friend. It was my crush on Georgie Dunn. I had planned on following him around all summer long until he noticed me. Now I wouldn't have the chance. So I argued and pleaded until I was blue in the face, but Mum wouldn't budge this time.

The very next Saturday some of Dad's relations, Cousin Harry and his big old wife Zelda, decided to make their annual one-day trek up to Muskoka. They said Dad and Arthur and I could ride for free in the rumble seat of their roadster. At least *that* sounded like fun. But it wasn't.

We had to leave at three in the morning to get there in time for breakfast. Well, it was so cold in the rumble seat that Arthur and I had to lie under a rug on the floor for the whole trip and Dad had to keep the rug from blowing off with his feet. It was the coldest I'd ever been in my life. It's a wonder we didn't get galloping pneumonia, if there is such a thing.

Arthur and I couldn't see a thing under the rug and we couldn't even talk for the noise of the wind and the tires. And the bumps on the road bounced us around and hurt something awful. All I could think about for the whole miserable journey was that my beautiful summer holidays would all be wasted and some other girl would be following after Georgie Dunn.

Aunt Aggie, who looked enough like me to be my mother, welcomed us with a whopping big breakfast. Even Grandpa Thomson, who Mum described as "an ugly man's dog if there ever was one," gave us a crooked smile and said he hoped I wouldn't eat him out of house and home.

Aunt Ida was there too. She was Dad's youngest sister and she had just recently separated from her husband, Uncle Wilbur. Well, in 1935 it was considered a pure disgrace to be separated so Aunt Ida had come up to her father's farm to try to live it down.

I didn't like her much. For one thing, she thought she was gorgeous. She had blonde, marcelled hair covered over with an invisible hairnet—which I could see as plain as day—and round blue eyes, and red bow-shaped lips. She wore floral, dimity frocks and high-heeled shoes and real silk stockings. And for another thing, she thought she was smart. She was forever showing off by reciting poetry: *Be good, sweet maid, and let who will be clever. Do noble things, not dream them all day long.* Every time she saw me she said those lines and I took it as a personal insult.

But I liked Aunt Aggie. She was a spinster and she stayed at home to help Grandpa work the farm. She was tall and lean and kind. Her straw-coloured hair was done up in a bun that looked like a cowflap and when she let it down at night it was long enough to sit on. Her face was lined and brown from the sun, and her bent-wire spectacles kept sliding down her shiny nose. She wore plain calico dresses, low-heeled house shoes and black cotton stockings that wrinkled around her ankles.

"Well, Bea, I like your new haircut," she said about my boyish bob. Mum had taken me down to Uncle Charlie's to have it cut that way so it would

6

last all summer and start to grow out just for school. I liked it myself because it was wash and comb and it made me feel like a boy.

Grandpa Thomson was old and stooped and grey. He had a wrinkled, leathery face and deep-set, piercing blue eyes. "You're getting to be a big girl, Beatrice," he said, and I took it as a compliment coming from him. It had been two years since I'd been up to Muskoka and he hadn't laid eyes on me in the meantime, so I guess I looked different to him. But as far as I could see I hadn't changed a bit. I was twelve-going-on-thirteen and I was still skinny as a rake and I hadn't even started to fill out where I was supposed to. Gladie had—and she was six months younger than me. That made me mad.

After we washed up the breakfast dishes we all trooped down to the barn to admire Bessie's brand-new calf. Grandpa let me name it and I called it Georgie even though it was a girl calf. Arthur called me a dumb-bell and I was afraid for a minute he'd guess about my crush on Georgie, but he didn't.

Then we all went to the back pasture to say hello to Major. He flung his head over the split-rail fence and nickered and nuzzled Arthur and me as if he remembered us. After that we followed Aunt Aggie to the hen house where she proudly counted out the laying hens. There were fourteen in all, sitting on their nests, chittering and blinking, their funny red eyelids going up instead of down. Clucking softly with her tongue, Aunt Aggie slipped a hand underneath each setting hen without disturbing it, and gathered some new-laid eggs to send back home to Mum.

Right after dinner, which was served at noon instead of supper time like at home, Cousin Harry jumped up and declared, "Well, we'd best be making tracks!" In spite of her broad backside wedged in the chair, Cousin Zelda was up like a shot and out the door leaving all the dirty dishes. (Cousin Zelda wasn't one of my favourite relations. She always said I was the dead-spit of Aunt Aggie, then in the next breath she'd say Aunt Aggie had a face like a horse's rear end.)

Dad kissed me goodbye and gave me a nickel to spend in case we ever went into Huntsville—which was very unlikely since Grandpa only had a horse and buggy and it would take all day to get there. Arthur thumbed his nose at me in a friendly way as he hopped into the rumble seat.

I watched as the roadster pulled away, swirling up the Muskoka dust, with Dad and Arthur waving gaily from the back.

A lump the size of a peach stone rose into my throat, nearly choking me. I waved and waved until they disappeared around the red-dirt turning and into the tunnel of trees. The red dust settled and I could see the heat waves rising from the road. A stream of loneliness washed over me and I felt as if I was going to drown.

Then Aunt Aggie hugged me from behind. I wheeled around and pressed my face against her warm, flat chest.

2
My hero

The log house had a big kitchen, a long parlour and
three bedrooms upstairs. I slept in the smallest bedroom on a narrow cot with a straw mattress. There
was a washstand beside the bed and a chamber pot
underneath it, that's all.

"This was your dad's room when he was a boy,"
Aunt Aggie reminded me. "The same bed too, mattress 'n all."

"And that's my grandmother in the picture," I
said, pointing to the likeness of a sad-faced woman
who looked a lot like me and Aunt Aggie.

"Yes, that's Ma. She died long before you were
ever thought of." Aunt Aggie kissed me on the forehead, blew out the candle and went downstairs.
(Grandpa Thomson didn't hold with taking lamps
upstairs just for getting into bed. Waste of kerosene,
he said.) Anyway, I could see by the moonlight coming in the little square window and it made me feel
less lonely sleeping in Dad's bed, with his mother
gazing down at me from the oval frame above.

I curled up and began to rub the knob on the end of my nose. It was Cousin Zelda who had told me that if I massaged the knob every night it would gradually wear away. She said she knew a girl who had a nose just like mine and after five years of massaging it she'd won a beauty contest. Not that I expected to win a beauty contest, but I was tired of having to face everybody all the time so they wouldn't notice my awful profile. And I thought that maybe without the knob I'd be good-looking like Arthur. We looked a lot alike, since we both favoured Dad's side, but he had a nice neat nose.

With the tip of my finger I rubbed in a circular motion, thinking about home. Things were going much better now that Dad was working steady. His pay packet was only twelve dollars a week, but Mum was really proud of how far she could make a dollar stretch. They didn't fight like they used to when Dad wasn't working and we were on the pogey. But they still couldn't afford more than one quart of milk a day so there was never enough for drinking, only for porridge and tea and hot-water cocoa.

Aunt Aggie knew this so she made sure I got lots of fresh milk while I was on the farm. Every day, morning and night, I'd follow her down to the barn with my cup. She'd fill it to the brim with foamy, warm milk right from the cow, laughing as she squirted the creamy jet dead centre into my cup. She said I reminded her of a heifer being fattened up for the slaughter. She said funny things, Aunt Aggie.

Every night she dosed me with a tablespoon of goose grease.

"Please! No more, Aunt Aggie!" I begged, backing away from the vile grey stuff heaped up on the spoon. "I'm all better now—honest!"

"Open your mouth and close your eyes," chanted idiotic Aunt Ida, "and you'll get something to make you wise."

"Just hold your nose and you won't taste it," Aunt Aggie advised.

"*No, please, Aunt Aggie!*"

At that Grandpa yanked off his earphones—he always listened to his crystal set before turning in—and barked, "Would you like me to hold your nose for you?"

So I gagged the goose grease down and went to bed and rubbed my nose, longing to be home. Tears trickled between my fingers as I thought about all the things I was missing—city noises like clanging trolleys, clopping horses, tin lizzies blaring *Ahhh-ooogah!* I missed the corner store and Sunnyside and the nickel matinee at the Lyndhurst too.

And Glad had written to tell me I had missed the best Sunday School picnic ever. It had been held at Centre Island and on the way home a terrible thunderstorm struck and a huge wave nearly washed a little boy right off the upper deck of the *Trillium*. Everybody got seasick, including the captain. And I missed it!

I missed my family most of all. Even Arthur. I missed the gang on Veeny Street, especially Georgie Dunn. I wondered if he even noticed I was gone.

THE SPORTING THINGS
For Young Folk to Wear

72-720
Blouse
8 to 14 yrs.
59c

3-piece
Linene
Sport
Outfit

72-721
Shorts
8 to 14 yrs.
69c

72-722
Skirt
8 to 14 yrs.
59c

Finally I fell asleep on my wet pillow, still thinking about Georgie and gagging on the goose grease.

But I guess the greasy cure was worth it because a few days later I woke up feeling terrific. "Can I go to the post office with you today, Aunt Aggie?" I asked as I cheerfully dried the noonday dishes.

I was dying to get to the post office because I was expecting a parcel. During my convalescence I had written lots of letters home—to Mum and Willa and Gladie and Grampa Cole.

In my letter to Mum I had begged her to send me a pair of summer shorts I'd seen in Eaton's catalogue one day while I was sitting in the backhouse. The winter catalogue was used up already and we had started on the summer one. Aunt Aggie said not to use the shiny coloured pages because they weren't very absorbent, so I was just idly leafing through the pictures when I spotted the shorts. The ad read: *For the Modern Miss. Navy blue shorts with jaunty red stripes down sides. Only 59¢, delivered.*

I could just see myself in those shorts at the Heckley Annual Picnic. I was pretty sure, if I got them, that I'd be the only girl there sporting the new-fangled style. I'd torn out the page, circled the picture and sent it off to my mum with a pleading letter.

Dearest Mum,

Today, in Eaton's catalogue, I found my heart's desire. *Shorts!* I need them right away in time for the Heckley Annual Picnic. If you send them I'll never ask for another thing as long as I live (or at least not for ages and ages).

Please excuse the shortness of this letter but Aunt Ida is going to the post office and she says she won't wait another minute. And you know Aunt Ida! But don't worry, I'll write again soon.

> With love from
> Booky

P.S.: Say hello to Dad for me, and kiss Billy, and maybe Jakey too, but not Willa and Arthur. Especially not Arthur! And don't forget my shorts!

> Your devoted daughter,
> Bea (Me!)

Back came Mum's postcard by return mail saying she'd get the shorts for me just as soon as she could scare up the fifty-nine cents. That was a week ago so I was sure they would have arrived by now.

Aunt Aggie hadn't answered my question about going to the post office yet and while she was thinking about it Aunt Ida butted in.

She had her head in the washbasin soaking her hair in lemon water to make it more blonde. Cocking her head to one side, she looked at me upside-down. "You're supposed to be here for your health, not to go gallivanting," she snapped.

Just then Grandpa came in carrying a bucket of well water in his gnarled old hand. When he saw the squeezed lemon halves lying on the washbench beside the basin he beetled his shaggy brows and growled, "That's a wicked waste of lemons."

Quick as a wink Aunt Ida thought up an excuse to justify herself. "I'm going to rub the pulp on my skin so it won't get all brown and freckled like Aggie's," she retorted.

Aunt Aggie's back stiffened and her eyes got a hurt look in them. "Some folks have to work for a livin'," she muttered. Then turning to me with a wry smile she said, "I have to help Pa hoe potatoes today, Bea, but I think you're old enough to go to the post office alone now, don't you?"

So away I ran down the road lickety-split, pleased as punch to be off by myself at last. Before I rounded the red-dirt turning I looked back to wave at Aunt Aggie, then headed into the tunnel of trees.

Heckley was the little hamlet nearest to Grandpa's farm. It was about a mile and a half down a wild and woodsy road. It had a pioneer stone church and a cemetery where Grandpa said most of his kinfolk were planted, an old log schoolhouse where Dad said he had learned the three Rs to "the tune of the hickory stick," ten houses and a post office.

The instant I walked into the post office Bertha Benchley, the postmistress (Aunt Ida said she was an evil old crone who read his Majesty's mail) hurried out from behind her wicket and handed me a parcel.

My heart leapt with joy. "Oh, boy! It's from my mother!" I cried ecstatically.

"Well, open it up and let's have a look-see," Bertha cackled as she obligingly cut the string.

I tore off the paper and out onto the floor fell the strangest thing—a pair of old, faded, baby-boy rompers. My heart sank to the soles of my running shoes.

"Well, dearie, what did you git from yer mother?" Bertha's wicked, toothless grin puzzled me for a minute.

"My mother . . . ?" I knew my mother would never play such a mean trick on me. Curious, I picked up the paper and looked at the address. The writing was unfamiliar, the stamps old and brittle. And there was no postmark. Suddenly I knew!

"You did this, Bertha Benchley!" My disappointment turned to blinding rage. "Aunt Ida is right. You're a disgusting old Nosey Parker who reads the King's mail and you ought to be arrested!" With that I threw the horrid rompers right in her repulsive face and slammed out the door.

Back on the road, I broke into a run. I sped past the houses of friends I had intended to visit, tears streaming down my face, with Bertha's witchy laughter echoing after me.

It seemed to take forever to reach the red-dirt turning. When it finally came into sight I saw that my path was blocked by a whole herd of black-and-white cows. I stopped short, and as if on signal they all turned their heads at once to glare at me.

I stood stock still, my heart banging against my ribs. The animals switched their tails, twitched their ears, chewed their cuds and swivelled their jaws. The one nearest me ran its long pink tongue right up its nose.

Oh, if only Aunt Aggie were here, I thought.

She'd know what to do. I had seen her elbowing her way nonchalantly through a herd of cows lots of times. She had told me repeatedly not to be afraid of cows because they were too dumb to even know that I was a different species, but those huge brown eyes looked smart enough to me. So I waited and waited... and they stared and stared. Finally, after standing still as a statue for ages and getting eaten alive by mosquitoes, I decided that the only way I could outsmart them was to cross the creek. So I took off my running shoes and began tiptoeing through the icy, marshy water.

Suddenly a stinging pain shot through my leg. I looked down and there, stuck to my skin like long, slimy blobs of glue, were two transparent pink things with red-and-blue veins showing through. Bloodsuckers! Vampires! Draculas!

All the terrifying stories I'd ever heard about leeches tumbled through my mind: one leech can drain all the blood from your body in ten seconds flat; two of them can do it in five seconds and leave you dead as a doornail!

Screaming like a banshee, I bolted out of the creek and flew around the turning, great clouds of red dust pluming up behind me as I raced for the house.

"They got me! They got me!" I shrilled, streaking into the kitchen like lightning. I pointed to my leg, which seemed to be shrivelling up before my very eyes.

"Eeek!" screeched Aunt Ida, jumping onto a chair and pulling her flowered skirt tight around her legs. "Beatrice Myrtle Thomson! Get those filthy things out of here this minute! Do you hear me?"

In answer I let out a bloodcurdling scream that brought Aunt Aggie and Grandpa galloping in from the far corner of the potato field.

One glance told Aunt Aggie what to do. Grabbing the salt-cellar off the table she unscrewed the cap and doused my leg with salt. The greedy devils devouring me writhed and wiggled like frosty dew-worms, but they wouldn't let go. So my brave Aunt Aggie, completely ignoring the fact that she could be sucked to death in five seconds flat, pinched them off with dirt-stained fingers and flung them out the door.

"There, there, Bea." She gathered me to her chest. "You're all right now."

Then she looked up at her hoity-toity sister, still perched on the chair. "Get down from there, you silly jackass!"

For a second there was dead silence. Then Aunt Aggie and I burst out laughing, and even Grandpa couldn't help but join us.

Jumping down from her perch, Aunt Ida swept us with a furious glare. "Fools!" she shrieked. Then, with her nose in the air, she clickety-clicked up the stairs, banging the stairwell door behind her.

I never did get my shorts. Mum's letter came a few days later explaining that she couldn't afford them this year. Maybe next year, she said.

I never forgave Bertha Benchley, even though she insisted it was all in fun.

But ever after that hectic day, Aunt Aggie was my hero.

3
Home again

When it came time to go home I didn't know whether to be glad or sorry. I had renewed all my old friendships with the kids in Heckley, and Grandpa had even started letting me ride Major. Bareback! When he saw how gentle the horse was with me and how much we loved each other, he even said I could ride him to the post office. But that only happened once because on the way home a car came along and spooked Major and he jumped the barbed-wire fence beside the road. I managed to hang on to his flying mane and I landed right on his back again, so there was no harm done, but Grandpa got mad as a tethered bull and roared at me furiously, "He might of broke his leg, you thoughtless wretch!" So I wasn't allowed to ride him off the farm anymore.

I had a wonderful time at the Heckley Annual Picnic too. Aunt Aggie and I won the three-legged race (I thought she'd kill me, dragging me along) but the prize was worth it—a little china horse that looked a lot like Major. And Aunt Aggie let me keep it. Then Aunt Ida won the shoe-kicking contest (no wonder, since her high-heeled slippers only weighed about half as much as those heavy clodhoppers the farm women wore) and her prize was a green glass candy dish she kept herself.

And what a supper we had! It was out of this world. There were salads and sandwiches and puddings and cakes and pies galore, and the women churned homemade ice cream right before our very eyes. It tasted heavenly.

Then Grandpa (who had been in a mood and hadn't spoken to a living soul in weeks) suddenly got over it and played the fiddle to beat the band at the after-supper barn dance.

To top it off, while I was sitting on an upturned barrel digesting my supper and enviously watching the square dancers, Horace Huxtable, whose sister Daisy was my best Muskoka friend, snuck up behind me, kissed me on the cheek and told me that he loved me. I nearly fell off the barrel and for a minute there I almost forgot about Georgie Dunn.

Anyway, after nearly two months in Muskoka I was getting lonely. Especially for the baby. Billy was only two and I was afraid he would forget me. Also, I was anxious to get home in time for Kid's Day at the Ex.

So Aunt Aggie began asking around Heckley to see if she could cadge me a ride to Toronto. I was hoping she'd succeed because I knew if Grandpa had to take me all the way in to Huntsville by horse and buggy and pay my fare on the train he'd be mad as hops.

He had a reputation for being stingy, Grandpa Thomson, and I could vouch for it. Why, he even called me a pig once just for asking for a second helping of blueberries. And I had spent the whole afternoon in the hot sun picking them all myself! ("Was Grandpa nicer when you and Dad were kids, Aunt Aggie?" I once asked her. I liked to think he was, and that he'd just got crabby with old age. But her nose screwed up and her specs slid down as she answered, "Does a leopard change its spots?")

Well, as it turned out, Horace Huxtable's Uncle Oscar had come up from Toronto one weekend and he said they could squeeze me in on the return trip. (Little did I know that they meant the word *squeeze* literally.) They were leaving Sunday afternoon so Aunt Aggie told me to go pack my grip.

That didn't take long because I didn't have much to pack. Besides my few clothes I had my china horse, some red chicken feathers to remind me of my pet rooster Reddy, and a shiny black bracelet I had braided myself out of Major's tail to remember him by.

That night I brought out my autograph book and asked my two aunts and my grandfather to each write a verse in it for me to remember them by. There were only a few empty pages left because everybody in Heckley had written in it. (Everybody except Bertha Benchley, that is. She offered to but I said no.)

Aunt Aggie's verse was cute and funny, like her:

Dear Bea,

Remember me when far away
And only half awake.
Remember me on your wedding day
And save me a piece of cake.

Lovingly,
Aunt Agnes

Aunt Ida's contribution was even worse than "*Be good, sweet maid*":

Beatrice,

If you wish to partake
Of heavenly joys,
Think more of your prayers
And less of the boys.

Sincerely,
Aunt Ida

Grandpa surprised me with a pretty piece of poetry:

Dear Granddaughter,

May your pathway through life
Be as happy and free,
As the dancing waves
On the deep blue sea.

Fondly,
Your Grandfather

Maybe he wasn't so bad after all.

I was to be picked up at three o'clock in the afternoon so first thing in the morning Aunt Aggie set a washtub full of rainwater out in the sun so it would warm up enough for me to take a bath right after dinner.

"I can't take my bath outside, Aunt Aggie!" I protested, horrified. "What if somebody sees me?"

"Who's going to look—the chickens?" she laughed.

She was right, of course. Nobody ever came that far along the road unless they were expected because there were no more farms beyond Grandpa's. And Grandpa was out in the field threshing and wouldn't be back until it was time to say goodbye.

The rainwater was soft and warm and deep and I was enjoying a good tubbing. I was washing myself with a flannel and the soap Aunt Aggie had made herself from her grandmother's recipe when I suddenly noticed that my chest was awfully tender and both sides were swollen.

"Aunt Aggie! Aunt Aggie!" I yelled in alarm. But Aunt Ida came instead.

"For mercy's sake, what is it now?" she asked irritably.

I had to tell her what I was yelling about but to my surprise her voice changed and became almost kind. "Oh, not to worry, Bea," she said with the pleasantest smile she'd ever bestowed on me. "It's just that you've begun to develop. You're turning into a woman, just like me."

Well, I was thrilled to be turning into a woman at last, but I hoped not just like her.

"Hurry up out of the tub and dry yourself off." She handed me a big piece of grey flannel. "I'll put a wave in your hair with my setting lotion."

That was the nicest thing Aunt Ida ever did for me, and it went a long way to making up for her natural nastiness.

My boyish haircut (I decided not to get it cut that way anymore, since I didn't want to be a boy after all) had grown out long enough for her to make a lovely deep wave. I sat out in the sun until it dried. Then she combed it out and fluffed it up and I couldn't get over myself. With my bright blue Thomson eyes and my deep suntan and my tawny wave dipping over my high forehead, I looked almost pretty in the mirror over the washbench. Even the knob on my nose seemed smaller. When I put on my clean dress and socks and shoes, Aunt Aggie said I looked cute as a bug's ear.

But the trip home was horrendous! I was squeezed into the back seat of an old tin lizzie with four other kids, all younger than me, and they carried on something awful. They threw up and wet themselves and cried and whined and pretty soon I was just as big a mess as they were. Then I'll be darned if we didn't pick up another passenger along the way, Norman Somebody-or-other, and he drank beer right out of a bottle and he kept pestering me for a kiss. So I shoved all the kids over beside him and stared out the window. I'd rather have been on the rumble-seat floor under a rug with Arthur any old day!

Well, after about a hundred stops to fix flat tires,

go to the bathroom beside the road and have a hotdog, we finally arrived at Veeny Street about midnight. I was so tired I thought I'd die.

Horace's Uncle Oscar banged on our front door and woke the whole neighbourhood up as well as Mum and Dad.

"Who is it?" Mum called from the upstairs window. Her voice was music to my ears.

"It's me, Mum, Booky!" I cried.

Then Dad came down in his underwear to let me in. He gave me a hug and went straight back upstairs to bed. He said he had to get up for work in a few hours. Mum kissed me and squeezed me and said I stunk to high heaven.

"I looked nice when I left, Mum, honest. I was all bathed and clean and Aunt Ida even waved my hair. But then those Huxtable kids got sick all over me and nearly made me sick too."

"Well, never mind. I'll make you some cocoa and then you can curl up on the davenport. Willa will never put up with the smell of you tonight. You can get cleaned up tomorrow."

Oh, it was nice sipping cocoa in my nightgown in our own kitchen with Mum.

"Your hair does look nice, Bea," Mum said. "Imagine old frosty-face fixing it for you."

The mention of Aunt Ida reminded me of what I wanted to tell my mum. "Guess what, Mum?"

"What, Bea?" She yawned sleepily.

"I've started to grow—right here." I patted my chest gingerly. "Aunt Ida says it's nothing to worry about. It's just that I'm becoming a woman. Isn't that swell, Mum? Aren't you glad?"

I drained my cup, then looked up, and to my amazement Mum's dark eyes were full of tears.

"What's the matter, Mum? Did I say something wrong?"

"No, no, Booky, it's nothing..." She dabbed at her eyes with her nightdress sleeve. Then she did the strangest thing. She drew me to her and gathered me onto her lap and held me close, whispering huskily, "My little girl...my baby..."

She hadn't called me a little girl in a month of Sundays, let alone a baby. And just when I was telling her about turning into a woman, too. Honestly, you never knew what to expect.

4
Grampa Cole

"Hi, Grampa! I'm home!" I poked my head inside Grampa Cole's kitchen door.

His back was to me, his tall, bony frame leaning over the stove. I smelled sausages and potato cakes sizzling in the black iron frying pan.

"Hallo, Be-*a*-trice!" He turned around, holding the lifter in mid-air, his faded brown eyes lighting up. "How's my girl?"

That's what I'd come to hear. That I was still his girl.

"I'm fine, Grampa, I'm all better now. I gained five pounds in Muskoka. Can you tell?" I lifted my arms and spun around.

"Now that you mention it, you do look bigger— and taller too."

"Where's Joey?" I peered past him into the dim, dark-panelled dining room. Joey was my boy-uncle, the youngest of Grampa's thirteen children. (Mum was the oldest.) Joey was jealous of me and Grampa so he always bullied me and chased me home.

"He's gone off fishing—won't be back till nightfall. So you'll just have to make do with me."

"I like it when there's just you and me." I hopped up onto Joey's stool beside the stove to watch Grampa turn the sausages and flip over the pancakes.

"Aye, it's nice, just you and me," he agreed, a little smile ruffling his ragged moustache. He never smiled a big smile. Mum said it was because he had no teeth. "Get the plates down, Bea, and help me eat this here grub." He gave the pan a final shake.

His dishes were kept on open shelves over the big white porcelain sink. They were discoloured and cracked with age.

"Mmm, it smells good." I smacked my lips as he slid two golden sausages and two crispy potato cakes onto each plate.

"Want some ketchup?"

"Store bought?"

"Yep. I got no homemade. Never turned my hand at preserving. When your Grandma was alive she used to make the spiciest ketchup you ever et."

"So does Mum. But I like store bought." I doused the bright red sauce all over the steaming food.

He poured us both a cup of tea from a smoky graniteware pot and laced it well with cream and sugar. Then he tipped some into his saucer, blew ripples across it and sipped it from the edge. I followed suit. Willa would have had a fit if she could have seen us. She said it was the height of ignorance, drinking from your saucer. Once in a while Dad would do it and when he did Mum would get mad and Willa would leave the table in disgust. Then Dad would holler after her, "If you don't like it here you can always pack your grip and leave!"

"How're Mr. Thomson's crops this year, Bea?"

"Oh, pretty good, I guess. But Aunt Aggie says nothing grows well that far north. Every year Grandpa puts in corn and it never gets big enough to pick before the frost." I paused to wash my food down with a big slurp of sweet tea. "Boy, Grampa, my other grandfather isn't half as nice as you."

"Well, Bea, it don't pay to judge a man till you've walked a ways in his boots."

"I guess. You want to know what happened to me, Grampa?" I prattled on and on, telling him all the news. He listened attentively, sipping from the saucer, his unkempt moustache floating in his tea. Finally I said, "You need a trim, Grampa."

His coarse, iron-grey hair grew thick as a bush all over his head and down the back of his neck, straggling over the collar of his blue-checked flannel shirt.

"Well, that's your job," he drawled.

Ever since I was a little kid I liked trimming his hair. He must have liked it too because he always let me do it; then the next day he would go to the barbershop to get it neatened up.

I tied a grey dishtowel around his scrawny, suntanned neck and reached for the scissors hanging on a nail on the side of the cupboard. "Want to light your pipe first?"

"Don't mind if I do."

He got his corncob from the window sill, clamped

it between his bare gums, struck a wooden match on the seat of his overalls and drew the flame, with a *putt-putt* sound, into the yellow bowl.

"Now hold still!" I commanded, and began my job. The wiry grey hair, tough as Major's tail, fell like bits of steel wool onto the towel.

"Tell me a story about when you were a boy, Grampa." His tales of the olden days always transported me back in time. "Tell me the one about Great-Aunt Gertrude."

"That one'll give you nightmares."

"I don't care. I like it." I shivered in anticipation.

"Well..." He closed his eyes, puffing his pipe, and the smoke wrapped softly around us. The mixture of smells that came from him—tobacco, wood smoke, sweat and axle grease—always lingered in my mind.

"It was this way," he began. "Great-Aunt Gertie was ninety-four years old and we had been expecting her to peg out for a long time. But when it finally happened it come as a shock, the way death always seems to do. Well, in those days there weren't no undertaker fellas. The womenfolk saw to the dead. So the neighbour ladies come to help my maither"—that's how Grampa said mother—"get the old lady ready. They laid her out in her Sunday best in a plain pine box in our parlour."

Putt-putt-putt went the pipe. *Crunch-crunch-crunch* went the scissors.

"Well, folks came from far and wide for the funeral, 'cause Great-Aunt Gertie was a Swansea pioneer and everybody knowed her for miles around. Pretty soon the parlour was overflowing and the menfolk had to stand up three deep along the back."

"Was it in this house, Grampa?" I leaned over backwards, peering through the creepy dining room into the gloomy parlour, half expecting to see the dark outline of a casket against the shuttered windows.

"No. I built this house for your Grandma and me when your maither was a baby. No, it was in my faither's house on the banks of the Grenadier. It's gone now. But in those days my faither's farm stretched all the way from High Park to Catfish Pond."

Putt-putt-putt. Snip-snip-crunch.

"Well, Reverend Ebenezer Stiles was preaching the service, and he just got to the part about what a fine upstanding Christian woman Great-Aunt Gertie was, when I thought I saw her fingers twitch—not much mind, just a mite. I darted a look at my maither and the rest of the family in the front row, but their eyes were all glued on the Reverend, so I guessed I was mistaken. He was a long-winded preacher, Reverend Stiles, and I was just a boy, so I begun to doze. Next thing I knew my maither was clutching my arm so hard I yelped. And ladies were fainting and the menfolk were gasping and Reverend Stiles was shouting, '*Praise the Lord, it's a miracle!*' And there, large as life and twice as ugly, sat Great-Aunt Gertie, bolt upright in her casket." He paused to tamp his pipe down and to strike another match. I was trimming the back of his neck and my hands were shaking so much I was afraid I'd pinch the loose skin between the blades.

"Go on, Grampa."

"Well, Great-Aunt Gertie stared straight ahead, looking neither to left nor to right, and cried out in a voice as clear as a bell, 'I want me tea!' Nobody moved. We was all transfixed. Then, before anybody had time to gather their wits and do her bidding, she fell back dead again."

A delicious shiver quivered up my spine. "Did she ever come alive again?" I whispered.

"Now you're gettin' ahead of me," he chided gently, then went on.

"Well, the Reverend cut his sermon short and shut the coffin lid with an unholy bang. And in the churchyard by the graveside, while he was saying 'ashes to ashes,' his eyes never strayed from that lid. It was as if he was expectin' it to pop open any second. But the planting went off without a hitch and afterwards, back at the house, there was a fine feast and a good time was had by all."

"Could that happen today, Grampa?"

"No, Bea, nowadays doctors use a modern gadget to check for heartbeats, and those undertaker fellas drain out every drop of blood to make certain that you're cold."

"Now tell me the one about the boy who climbed out of his coffin in the middle of the night and went outside to fix his wagon and lived to be a hundred. Boy! Those sure were the good old days, Grampa."

"No, Bea, those were bad old days. Things are better now." He held out his pipe at arm's length while I trimmed the tea stains off his moustache. Then I undid the towel and shook it out the door.

"Well, that's all the storytellin' for now. I think

I'll take a snooze. I cut a stack of wood this mornin' and I'm all done in."

"Okay, Grampa. Thanks for the story. I'm going to go home and write it down so I won't forget it."

"You'll have a hard time forgettin' that one. I think you know it better than I do." He lay down on the day bed under the dining-room window and I kissed him goodbye under his scratchy moustache.

Back home I rummaged through my schoolbag, found an empty workbook and wrote the story down as fast as my pencil would fly. Such eerie tales so sparked my imagination that I made up a gruesome one of my own about a man who had been buried alive. When he was dug up by grave robbers they found his hands full of hair because he had gone mad and torn himself bald. So the grave robbers learned their lesson and reformed and became just plain thieves.

When I was finished I ran out the front door to see if any of our gang was hanging around Veeny Street.

A bunch of little kids—my brother Jakey and Florrie and Skippy and Katie—were playing kick-the-can, so I rounded them up and made them sit in a row along the curb. Then I saw Ada and Ruthie coming out of Hunter's Grocery Store on the corner. So I hollered, "Hurry up, you two, I'm going to read a story!" They both sat down, looking kind of skeptical. Then Arthur came out of our house and Gladie and her brother Buster came out of their house to see what was going on. I read them the stories, with lots of acting out and expression, and at the end Florrie and Skippy ran home screaming their heads off.

"I'm telling Mum on you, Bea!" Jakey's big brown eyes were glistening and his round face was as white as toilet paper.

"Those are dumb stories," declared Arthur, marching off.

"You're weird, Bea, you really are." Ruthie got up huffily, brushing the back of her skirt.

"They're not real stories," sniffed Ada, her bottom lip trembling. "They're not even printed. You just made them up."

"I did not! They're true as life. You can ask my grandfather," I shot back indignantly.

Even Gladie looked perturbed. "You're going to get in trouble, Bea," she whispered.

But her big brother, Buster, was exuberant. "Boy! Those are the best ghost stories I ever heard, Bea. Do you think you could memorize them for the corn roast down at the Camel's Back on Saturday night? It'll be too dark outside to read."

Just then Dad bellowed out the door, "Beatrice! You get yourself in here!"

Jakey had told on me, and Skippy's mother had come through the lane to our back door hopping mad, complaining that I had scared Skippy into hysterical fits. So Dad gave me a good tongue-lashing and sent me to bed without my supper. Then, about half-an-hour later, the door creaked open and Arthur shoved in a brown-sugar sandwich. Arthur, of all people! As Mum would say, wonders never cease.

I considered myself lucky to be let off without a razor-stropping, which was how Dad usually punished us for serious offences. So to take my mind off my stomach I recited the stories over and over while massaging the end of my nose, and by the time I went to sleep I knew them off by heart.

Then on Saturday night with the dancing orange flames of the bonfire casting ghostly shadows all around us, I acted out my scary stories in my creepiest voice and I was a huge success. Even Arthur and Willa joined in the applause and I was pleased as punch with myself because I'd never been the centre of attention before. And Georgie clapped and whistled and said my stories were the scariest of the whole night. Then to top it off he asked if he could walk me home; but just then Arthur interrupted and cranky old Willa insisted that I get home because it was past my bedtime. So Georgie went with Arthur and Buster and I walked home with Willa, my perfect evening ruined.

5
Senior Fourth

Mum let me wear my best dress for my first day in Senior Fourth. Now that Dad was working steady (touch wood—he'd been worried lately about layoffs at the factory) I had three dresses: a blue taffeta for Sundays, a blue cotton for school and a faded blue calico playdress. Blue was my favourite colour. Today I was wearing my taffeta.

The week before school started Willa had bought me a bottle of green Hollywood Waveset out of her own money. So I practised setting my wave for a whole week and I finally got it perfect.

I walked across Veeny Street instead of running lickety-split, not wanting to disturb my wave. The brown sandy road had been freshly oiled to keep the dust down but the little kids had sprinkled a dirt path from one side to the other. I picked my way carefully across the zigzaggy path to Gladie's house so as not to track black oil onto the floors.

I was allowed to walk right into her house without knocking. Aunt Ellie, Gladie's pleasant mother, said that with so many chickens of her own in the nest, one more didn't make any difference.

As I came in the door she was straining her ears to hear Jim Hunter's news broadcast over CFRB while all the kids were scurrying around getting ready for school.

We didn't have a radio in our house. Dad said he didn't need a radio to tell him that times were bad, and he didn't want that blatherskite R.B. Bennett bellowing his lies in our front room. Dad blamed Prime Minister Bennett for the Depression, so I guess that's why he was a blatherskite. But if Mum had her way we'd have a radio—it was one of the wonders of the modern world, she said.

Sometimes I went over to Gladie's house to listen to the daytime serials. My favourite was *Our Gal Sunday.* Every day it started out with the same question: *Can a girl from a small mining town in the West find happiness as the wife of a wealthy and titled Englishman?* Boy, I thought, I bet *I* could if I had the chance. But day after day the question was left up in the air and we never did find out the answer.

"Bye, Mum!" Gladie called over the din.

"Bye, Aunt Ellie!" I echoed.

"Toodle-oo, you two, mind your p's and q's!"

Outside Gladie said, "You look swell, Bea. Sort of different and grown up."

"Gee, thanks, Glad." I decided to drop the 'ie' from her name because it suddenly sounded babyish. "You look nice too." And she did. She had shiny black hair, sparkling brown eyes and even white teeth. Mum said Glad was a dyed-in-the-wool Cole.

"Senior Fourth is pretty nearly grown up, you know, Glad. That's as far as my mother ever went in school; then she got a job at Eaton's. But she says all us kids have to go to high school. She says if you want to get anywhere in this world you need an education. Oh, gosh, Gladie—Glad—how am I ever going to do Senior Fourth arithmetic?"

Arithmetic had been the bane of my existence ever since my first day in school. That day Mrs. Gumm, my Junior First teacher, had stood up in front of the class brandishing a big, thick ruler, and had announced to all us quivering kids that the first one to make a mistake would get the ruler over his knuckles. Then she looked straight at me and bellowed, "You! What's one plus one?"

Well, Willa had taught me one *and* one long ago, but I didn't know what 'plus' meant, so I burst out crying and *crack* came the ruler over my skinny little fingers. I had been terrified of arithmetic ever since.

"Oh, for Pete's sake, Bea, quit worrying. I'll help you," promised Gladie.

Her confidence cheered me up, for the time being anyway. Lucky for me she was good in arithmetic.

About a block from the school we heard the warning bell that meant it was five minutes to nine. We broke into a run, me cupping my hands protectively over my wave. In the schoolyard we joined the rest of the girls in our gang. They were all nervous and excited and talking a mile a minute.

Clang went the bell. Mr. Davidson, the school

principal, held the big iron bell in one hand and hit the clapper inside of it with the other.

On the first clang we froze as if playing statues. The second sent us scurrying to our lines. Then he clanged the bell rhythmically: *clang,* march, *clang,* march, *clang,* march, right into our classrooms.

There were two Senior Fourths in Swansea School that year. Mr. Bewdley, who had a reputation for being a terrible tyrant, and Mr. Jackson were the teachers. Gladie and I were both lucky enough to be in Mr. Jackson's class.

He was leaning on his desk when we entered the room, one hand nonchalantly in the pocket of his blue serge suit. He was tall, dark and handsome— just like Ramon Novarro, the movie star whose framed picture Willa had on our bedroom wall.

All during Junior Fourth I had worshipped him from afar. And now, like a dream come true, he was going to be my teacher for a whole year. Maybe two, if my luck ran out.

"You may sit anywhere you like for the time being," he said, his rich baritone voice sending shivers up my spine. Glad and I made a mad scramble for the front seat right under Mr. Jackson's perfect nose.

He waited patiently for the shuffling and rustling to stop. Then, flashing a glittering smile, the like of which I'd never seen except in an Ipana toothpaste ad, he said, "Good morning, ladies and gentlemen."

"Good morning, sir!" we chorused in delight.

"The rest of the pupils in Swansea School are boys and girls," he continued. "Children. You might

even call them kids if you're partial to baby goats."
We rippled with appreciative laughter. "But everyone in *my* class is a young man or a young woman
on the threshold of adulthood. *You* are Seniors!" He
waved his hand dramatically across the room. "I
intend to treat you like Seniors. And I expect you to
act like Seniors."

This incredible news worked like a charm. We all
sat up straighter, wiped the grins off our faces and
tried our best to look like adults.

Going behind his desk he pulled open the top
drawer, took out the dreaded strap and very deliber-
ately dropped it with a *clunk* into the wastepaper
basket. "Adults do not require spankings," he said.
And that's the last we ever saw of the strap.

Now he sat down at his desk and rested his chin
on his slender, folded hands. Gladie and I sighed
blissfully in unison.

"I always like to start the new school year by
getting acquainted," Mr. Jackson was saying. "I'm
going to pass out foolscap and I want you to tell me
all about yourselves." He went up and down the
aisles passing out paper and talking as he went. "For
instance, what are your future plans? Have you any
hobbies? Or perhaps you'd like to tell me how you
spent your summer. What did you do with those
two glorious months of freedom? Tell me in your
own words and in your own way. And we won't
worry about spelling and neatness today. This is not
an examination. No marks will be lost for errors."

While I waited for my paper I sucked the oil off
my new pen nib and soaked it in the inkwell of the
freshly varnished desk. There were a few things I

liked about school—new pen nibs, full inkwells and blank foolscap just begging to be written on. I could hardly wait to get started. Everything that had happened to me in Muskoka that summer came tumbling into my mind: the leeches nearly sucking me to death, riding Major, Horace Huxtable actually stealing a kiss. I wrote small and fast, filling both sides of the page and even running up and down the margins.

"Yours is awful messy, Bea," whispered Gladie. Hers was neat enough to be entered in a penmanship contest. But her page was only half full.

"Well, he said neatness doesn't count this time," I reminded her. Then the person at the back of the row collected all the papers and gave them to Mr. Jackson.

After recess Mr. Jackson passed out more supplies. We sharpened our pencils and wrote our names on our workbooks. Gladie and I managed to get all our stuff packed into the one desk we shared. At twelve o'clock sharp the bell rang and we went home for dinner.

During dinner I asked Mum if she thought I could be a teacher if I really put my mind to it.

"Well, Bea, you'll have to work a lot harder than you've done in the past." She turned to Billy and wiped the honey off his cute face and untied the shoestrings of his little black boots.

"I will, Mum, I promise. Gee, I can hardly wait to get back to school this aft'."

"Well, by Jove, that's a good sign," she laughed.

"Bea-Bea!" Billy stretched out his long, skinny arms to me. "I want you!" He'd been saying that

41

and clinging to me like flypaper ever since I'd come home from Muskoka.

"Fat chance of him ever forgetting you," Mum said.

"I'll take him up to bed, Mum," I volunteered, scooping him up and squashing him in my arms. He was nearly three years old and really too big for me to carry now, but I still liked to. I staggered up the stairs with his long, gangly legs hanging down past my knees. He was going to be tall and slim like Grampa Cole.

"You missed Bea-Bea, didn't you, Billy?" I kissed him all over his sweet face, then heaved him, with a loud grunt, over the railing of the old iron cot. "But I'm in a hurry today—so bye-bye!" I left him wailing indignantly, expecting me to jiggle his cot like I always did until he went off to sleep.

Seven-year-old Jakey, who was in Senior First this year, was standing by the door crying his eyes out because he didn't want summer to be over.

"You go with Bea, Jakey," Mum said, smoothing the dark curls off his forehead. "There's a good boy. I've got to get done while Billy's in bed." Poor Mum. She was always trying to get done.

"Do I *have* to take him this year, Mum?" I looked down without a twinge of pity at his round, tear-stained face. "He's big enough to go by himself now."

"I haven't got time to argue!" she snapped.

I decided I'd better take him. The school was only a hop, skip and a jump down the street and I'd be rid of him as soon as we got there because he had to go in on the boys' side.

"Bye, Mum!" I called through the screen door.

"Bye, Booky. Be good."

"Mum . . ."

"What is it now?"

"Don't call me Booky anymore, okay? It sounds too babyish and Mr. Jackson says we Seniors are on the threshold of adulthood."

"Oh, all right," she laughed, "but you'll always be Booky to me."

Up until then I'd always liked my special little nickname. Maybe I'd tell her it was okay as long as we were in the house.

The afternoon was as interesting as the morning. At recess Gladie and I were leaning back-to-back in the schoolyard, holding each other up and talking over our shoulders.

"Isn't Mr. Jackson terrific?" I said. "Doesn't he remind you of Ramon Novarro or Robert Taylor?"

"Yah!" Gladie agreed, the same note of rapture in her voice.

"Or maybe Gary Cooper. Did you see *Lives of a Bengal Lancer?*"

"I wonder if he's married?"

"Who? Gary Cooper?" I asked.

"No! Mr. Jackson."

"Oh, gosh, I hope not!" The thought really upset me. "Because I think I'm in love with him and it wouldn't be proper if he was married."

"Well, I'm in love with him too." Gladie stepped away all of a sudden and nearly let me fall on the ground.

"Not as much as I am though." I scrambled to regain my balance.

"Oh, Bea!" Gladie scoffed. Then the bell rang and

saved us from having a fight.

The truth of the matter was, almost every girl in Senior Fourth had a crush on Mr. Jackson and the Georgie Dunns and Horace Huxtables of the world couldn't hold a candle to him.

After recess Mr. Jackson gave us back our marked compositions and I got ninety-two percent. I couldn't get over it!

"Your essays were of a very high calibre," he told the whole class, "and a few were so exceptional I'd like to hear them read out loud. We'll begin with Beatrice Thomson's."

I nearly sank through the floor. I felt a red flush spread up my face and creep under my stiff blonde wave.

Instantly my gallant teacher recognized my distress and came to my rescue. "Perhaps you'd like me to do the honours today, Beatrice, and you can favour us another time?"

So he did. He read my composition with such wonderful expression and enthusiasm that it sounded like a real story out of a book. The other kids all laughed at the funny parts and clapped their hands at the end.

Placing the foolscap back on my desk he said, "You have a fine flair for words, Beatrice. You show real potential. Keep up the good work."

I stared up at him in dumbfounded adoration. Never before in all my school life had a teacher complimented or encouraged me. It was one of the happiest days of my life. And it was a turning point. Never again did I feel quite so scatterbrained, or homely, or just plain dumb.

6
Our Arthur's birthday

On Arthur's birthday Mum said he could have a friend over for supper.

"When it's my birthday can I have somebody over too, Mum?"

"We'll see," she said, whipping the chocolate icing vigorously with a fork. "What with your birthday and Billy's landing on the same day it makes it kind of hard, but we'll see." Billy had been born on my tenth birthday so I always considered him my special birthday present.

My mouth began to water as Mum made chocolate swirls all over the top and sides of the double-layered cake. "Who's Arthur having for supper, Mum?"

She was poking blue candles in the peaks around the cake's circumference. "Oh, just Georgie Dunn," she said.

Just Georgie Dunn! The news made me forget all about asking to lick the icing bowl. Instead I bolted up the stairs, two at a time, to the bathroom.

Jakey was standing on a little stool, splish-splashing in the sink the way little kids do.

"Beat it, Jakey!" I commanded. "I need the bathroom."

"Do you have to go bad?" he asked.

"Yes," I lied, shoving him out the door. Latching it behind him I took a good look at myself in the mottled mirror hanging over the sink. I was a mess! My wave had fallen out, I had a ripe pimple on my chin and my neck was dirty.

I took the cake of carbolic soap from the wire drip-cage suspended between the taps and gave myself a thorough sponging. Then I cleaned my teeth with baking soda. (There was no toothpaste, but now that Dad was working steady we each had a toothbrush. Mine was blue.) Next I squeezed the pimple and it came out clean as a whistle. Then, using the big white family comb, I set my corn-coloured hair with green Hollywood lotion. My boyish bob had grown out long enough, at last, to make a kiss-curl in front of each ear as well as a deep wave over my left eye.

On the shelf beside the baking soda sat a jar of vaseline for cuts and scrapes. I smeared some on my finger and held it under my eyelashes. Then I fluttered my sparse, fair lashes up and down against my finger the way I'd seen Mum's sister, Auntie Gwen, do, and pretty soon they were all wet and shiny and glued together. Instantly my eyes looked bigger and bluer.

Next I went to Willa's and my bedroom and got my second-best dress out of the closet. It had a white piqué collar and cuffs. (Mum had made it for me from a twenty-five-cent remnant she got on sale at Eaton's.) I found clean white socks in my drawer and put them on with my black patent-leather shoes.

Then I spotted Willa's lip rouge standing on the bureau beside her Pond's Vanishing Cream. Every night she slathered on the cream, hoping to make her freckles disappear, but they never did. The lip rouge was "Tangee Natural." I had often been tempted to use it but I had never had the nerve before. Pulling my lips taut against my front teeth, I smoothed it on and pressed my lips together. They weren't red enough so I did it again. Instantly my teeth looked whiter and the gaps between them didn't seem so wide.

Next I went to my parents' bedroom at the back of the house. Raising the window, I put the stick in place to hold it up and stuck my head out to let the setting sun dry my hair.

Ruthie Vaughan was in her back yard next door playing roundabout against their house with her India rubber ball. "Hi, Bea!" she called up to me. I said hi. She threw the ball against the imitation-brick siding, did a twirling roundabout that billowed out her red plaid kilt, and caught the ball on the rebound. "How come you're hanging out the window?" she asked.

"Oh, just for a breath of air," I answered.

"Well, c'mon out, why don'tcha?"

"Can't. I got to help my mother lay the table. It's our Arthur's birthday and he's having Georgie Dunn over for supper."

An expression of pure envy flitted across her face.

Quick as a wink she wiped it off, tossed her curly brown hair, cried "Well, whoop-dee-do!" and went back to playing roundabout.

I felt my wave to see if it was dry. Not quite, even though the sun was unusually warm for October. Dad said it was Indian summer. The leaves had begun to turn and I could see flecks of gold shimmering on top of Grampa Cole's soft maple. His yard backed onto ours, separated by a laneway. I hadn't been over to visit him lately and I missed him, seeing his tree.

I'll go over tomorrow, I promised myself. And I'll explain how busy I am in Senior Fourth. (I did my homework every night now—I'd do anything for Mr. Jackson.) I knew Grampa would understand because we were kindred spirits.

Just to the north of Grampa's place I could see the red and green leaves of Billy and Maude Sundy's big old oak tree. I'll visit Billy and Maude soon too, I thought. They must wonder what's become of me. Our landlord and landlady were my best grown-up friends. They were brother and sister and they'd never been married so they lived together. Imagine growing up and having to live with your brother! I'd rather eat dirt than live with Arthur.

Finally my wave was dry so I pulled my head back in, took out the stick and lowered the window.

Back in our bedroom I combed out my hair, put on some more Tangee and slipped my horsehair bracelet over my bony wrist. I didn't own any jewellery but the glossy black hairs from Major's tail matched my patent leather shoes exactly. Glancing in the mirror, I noticed that my dress was getting tight across my chest so I decided I'd have to hold my breath for the rest of the day. But generally speaking I was quite tickled with myself. Even my nose didn't look too bad. I went downstairs singing "You oughta be in pitchers . . . "

Mum had already set the round dining-room table with the white cloth and the good dishes. The table looked pretty with the chocolate cake in the middle. I counted the candles to make sure there were fifteen. Boy, Arthur was getting old!

"Help me put the chairs around, Bea," Willa said. Then she took a closer look at me and let out a big screech. "Bea! You rat! You've got my lip rouge on! How dare you touch my Tangee? You'll get germs all over it!"

"Oh, Willa, please . . . " If she made a scene in front of Georgie Dunn I'd die. "I won't do it again, honest, but please, *please,* don't be mad this time."

I could tell by the way her stern expression softened that she had guessed why I'd fixed myself up. "Oh, all right. I'll let you off this time. But don't you dare do it again. Tangee costs money, you know."

"I know. And I'll be eternally, perpetually grateful!" I promised fervently.

"Oh—you and your big words!" she scoffed, but not nastily. I used a lot of big words since Mr. Jackson had told me I had a flair.

Dad brought Billy's beat-up old high chair in from the kitchen, and when he saw me he frowned and said, "What's that warpaint doing on your face, Missy?" But I could tell he wasn't really mad by the little smile that played around his mouth.

Mum came in to see what all the fuss was about. She took one look at me and exclaimed, "My stars, Bea! Aren't you a bit young for that?"

"Oh, please, Mum, let me wear it just this once. Willa says it's all right." I knew what Willa said went a long way with Mum.

"Oh, well, what's the harm?" She laughed and pinched my nose shut. "It's a special occasion, and the colour suits you."

"Gee, thanks, Mum. Can I wear lipstick to Sunday School too if Willa lets me?"

"Mercy me, no! Give you an inch and you want a mile!"

Just then Arthur and Georgie came in the front door, laughing and poking each other.

"Sit yourselves down," Mum told them. "Bea, you and Willa can help me carry."

We had roast beef and gravy and peas and carrots and mashed potatoes, and it wasn't even Sunday. But of course it *was* Arthur's birthday.

I don't know whether it was just plain luck or what, but I found myself sitting next to Georgie. I kept glancing at him out of the corner of my eye. (I had a bit of trouble doing this because the vaseline stuck my lashes together and I had to open my eyes wide to unstick them.) Georgie was even handsomer than Arthur. He had sparkly blue eyes, curly black hair and a dimple in his chin.

"How's school, Bea? I hear you got Daddy Long-Legs this year."

"Oh, no!" His sudden question took me off guard and I got all flustered by his sparkly eyes. "I got Mr. Jackson and he's terrific!" Everybody laughed and my face went beet red as I realized that Mr. Jackson's nickname was Daddy Long-Legs.

"Well, how's Senior Fourth anyway?" continued Georgie, just as if I hadn't said a really dumb thing.

"It's great!" I tried to control the quaver in my voice. "And Mr. Jackson says I've got potential."

"Oh, for gosh sakes, Bea, why do you have to tell that to everybody?" said Arthur scornfully. "I must have heard it a million times already."

"You're just jealous," I taunted, spurred on by Georgie's attention.

"Jealous of *you?* Don't make me laugh!"

Mum glared at us and changed the subject before Dad had time to get riled. He had been in a bad mood lately and the long hours at the factory—ten hours a day, six days a week—were beginning to tell on him.

"Tell your mother to come over and have tea with me sometime, Georgie," Mum continued. Then Dad asked him how his father was making out with his new job at the Bolt Works.

When it came time for the cake Dad lit the candles with a wooden match and Willa turned the lights off. That was the moment I loved, with the circle of faces all aglow in the candlelight.

"Make a wish, Arthur!" Mum's eyes rested lovingly on her eldest son's bright face and I felt a stab of jealousy. Sometimes I was sure that Arthur was Mum's favourite.

Billy and Jakey started to huff and puff impatiently and Dad said, "Settle down, you two." He had to relight two of the candles.

We all sang "Happy birthday, dear Arthur." Then

he took a deep breath and blew out all the candles at once. Dad turned on the lights and Mum sliced the cake.

Throughout the meal I had been sneaking more looks at Georgie and the last time our eyes met he winked at me. I nearly keeled off the chair. It was the first time in my life I could only eat one piece of cake.

Afterwards Arthur opened his presents. I gave him an art pencil with an eraser on it because he was going to be an artist.

"Thanks, Bea. I can really use it," he said. That was the nicest thing he'd said to me since I could remember.

Willa gave him a drawing pad; Dad and Mum gave him oxfords; Jakey and Billy gave him a card they'd made themselves. Georgie gave him a penknife with all sorts of attachments. Arthur was thrilled with it.

When the table was cleared he suggested a game of euchre. Willa jumped up and got the cards out of the sideboard drawer. She loved euchre.

When we cut the cards for partners I got Georgie and we won three games out of five. Willa and Arthur were fit to be tied.

Then Mum came in from the kitchen with the rest of the cake and some hot cocoa. While we were eating Georgie happened to notice my bracelet. "Where did you get it?" he asked.

"It's in memoriam of Major, my grandfather's horse," I explained. "I braided it myself out of his tail."

"Is he dead?" asked Georgie.

"Who, Grandpa?"

"No, the horse."

"No, why?" I was getting bewildered.

"Oh, Bea," chided Willa. "Don't show your ignorance."

"I thought you were supposed to be so smart with words," snorted Arthur. "Any dumb-bell knows that 'in memoriam' means in memory of somebody who's dead."

My face blazed with embarrassment and I couldn't speak for the lump that popped into my throat.

"Well, it's a unique bracelet anyway," said Georgie. I never dreamed a boy could be so nice.

At ten o'clock Georgie had to go home. "Thanks for the good time, Mrs. Thomson," he said politely while putting on his cap. "The supper was terrific. Especially the cake."

Mum just beamed. "Go out the front door, Georgie," she said. "My father always says the back door is only for tramps and peddlers."

I ran ahead of him to open the front door. On his way out he said, "Bye, Bea. Be seeing you."

Be seeing you! No boy had ever said that to me before!

"My, that Georgie Dunn turned out nice," Mum said as she tidied up the table. "And to think I used to call him a Peck's Bad Boy."

I went to bed in a daze with "Be seeing you" ringing in my ears. Boy, was I glad I'd been in Muskoka so I hadn't tried to follow Georgie around until he noticed me. It was like Mum always said: bad beginnings make good endings.

7
White Smock

My thirteenth birthday, and Billy's third, landed on a Saturday. We couldn't do any celebrating though, because both Billy and Jakey had the chicken pox. But I did get some wonderful presents.

Willa gave me my own Tangee. "So you can keep your germs to yourself," she said without cracking a smile.

Arthur gave me a pretty beaded comb. "So *our* comb won't be full of green jelly all the time," he joked.

And Mum gave me the best present of all—a permanent wave. "I've made an appointment for you at the Fair Lady Beauty Parlour on Bloor Street, Booky," she said, rubbing her palms together in that excited way she had. "Now what do you say to that?"

"Oh, Mum!" I flung my arms around her neck and gave her a big smacker. "Thanks profoundly!"

"Well, don't forget to thank your father profoundly too. He did without carfare all week to save the money for you."

"Gee, thanks, Dad." I kissed him too, but more shyly, because Dad wasn't much of a kisser.

"Well, thirteenth birthdays don't come a dime a dozen," he remarked drily.

Right after our noonday meal Mum gave me two dollars and fifteen cents. "On your way home I want you to stop at the butcher shop and get fifteen-cents' worth of stewing beef for Sunday supper." She tied the money securely in my hanky. "Now don't lose it. There's no more where that came from."

I shoved the hanky deep into the pocket of my old winter coat and did up the top two buttons. Dad said it had turned cold overnight.

"That coat's way too short," Mum remarked, spinning me around for inspection. "My stars, Bea, ever since you got back from Muskoka you've been growing like a burdock."

At the corner of Veeny and Mayberry streets I saw Gladie coming out of Hunter's Grocery Store. "Hi, Bea. Where you going?"

"Oh, just to Bloor to get something for my mother." I was hoping against hope she wouldn't offer to come with me because I wanted my permanent wave to be a complete surprise. As far as I knew, no other girl in Senior Fourth had a permanent wave.

"Gee, I'd come with you but I have to go straight home and mind Florrie."

"That's too bad." I tried to sound disappointed. "See you later then."

I was so preoccupied, imagining how swell it was going to be not having to set my hair with green lotion anymore, that I bumped smack into Roy-Roy the dumb boy.

"S'cuse me!" I said, then, "Oh, hi, Roy-Roy!" I always tried to treat him like a normal kid because Mum had told me, what with Raggie-Rachel for a mother and no brains to speak of, Roy-Roy had a hard row to hoe.

"Ha, ha, Bea-Bea!" His big hazy-blue eyes lit up and his wide mouth gaped open in a huge, wet grin. Rivers of slobber ran down his chin, soaking his flannelette bib.

We walked along together for a way, Roy-Roy hopping beside me with his peculiar, gangly gait, his long arms flailing the air in an effort to make me understand his gabbling.

I managed to catch something about a dog and a rabbit, and we were just starting to make some headway in the conversation when his mother's shrill voice shrieked at us out of nowhere. *"Roy-Roy! You git home this minute or I'll skin you alive!"*

Our heads jerked up simultaneously. There she sat on the upstairs window ledge of the Ashton's house, cleaning the top window pane. Sometimes Raggie-Rachel did chores like that to earn a bit of money. *"Git! Git! Git!"* she screeched.

Each "git" was punctuated by a snap of the cleaning rag. Clouds of Dutch Cleanser billowed out around her tattered bottom. It was funny, I thought, that Roy-Roy was always dressed much better than his mother.

The poor boy was so terrified he shook like a leaf; the slobber flew in every direction.

"You leave my boy alone, girl, you hear!" Her

face was livid and she shook her fist so hard I expected her to come tumbling out the window.

"I was only talking to him!" I dared to yell back at her because I knew she couldn't get at me from way up there.

"Well, he cain't talk, so don't you think you can fool Rachel Butterball!" (Her last name was really Butterbaugh, but everybody, including herself, pronounced it Butterball.) "I know all you smart-alecky kids make fun of my boy."

"Baa-baa, Bea-Bea!" Roy-Roy staggered frantically backwards, his wobbly legs going every which way.

"Bye-bye, Roy-Roy!" I ran backwards too and we kept on waving in spite of his mother shaking a Dutch Cleanser tempest all over the place.

I walked soberly the rest of the way, reflecting on how lucky I was. Sure, my family had been hard hit by the Depression. We'd gone hungry and cold lots of times. Once we'd even been put out of our house in the middle of the night. All the same, I felt rich beside Roy-Roy. Imagine having to live in a tar-paper shack down by Catfish Pond with a terrible mother like Raggie-Rachel. Poor Roy-Roy.

I was still half an hour early for my appointment when I got to Bloor Street so I decided to get Mum's meat first. The bell jangled overhead as I pushed open the heavy butcher-shop door. While I waited my turn I scraped up a pile of sawdust between my feet. It smelled nice and piney—like the woodshed behind the house in Muskoka.

"What can I do for you, Bea?" asked the butcher, wiping his bloody fingers on his white coat.

"Fifteen-cents worth of stewing beef with some extra suet, please, Mr. Donnan." Immediately I began working the knot of my hanky undone. He waited patiently until I put the money in his hand. We ran a bill at Hunter's Grocery Store, but Mr. Donnan said he wouldn't give so much as a soup bone on tick. He said he'd been stung more times than a bear in a beehive.

I watched him slice up the meat on the big wooden chopping block. One of the fingers on his left hand was missing and I tried not to think about it, but I couldn't help wondering who ate it.

I was still a little early when I got to the Fair Lady so I sat down on a wicker chair to wait. I put the package of meat on the window sill in the draught to keep it cool.

Strange smells drifted up from the back of the shop—sort of perfumy-mediciny smells all mixed together. Craning my neck around the archway I could see ladies' crossed legs sticking out.

Minutes passed and no one bothered with me, so I picked up a dog-eared *Silver Screen* from a messy, cigarette-burned table. Janet Gaynor and Charles Farrell were on the cover, his smooth dimpled cheek nestled into her curly brown hair. Could anybody be that beautiful? I wondered. Inside was a full-page picture of Tom Mix and his wonder horse, Tony. He was my favourite cowboy star but I hadn't seen his latest serial because I couldn't get a nickel for the Saturday matinee at the Lyndhurst.

I turned the page and was admiring a darling picture of Shirley Temple in her costume for *The Little Colonel* when a tall lady in a white smock appeared in the archway. She had peroxide-blonde hair and bright red lips that were bigger than her mouth.

"What do you want?" she snapped.

"My mum made me an appointment for a permanent wave." I held out the crumpled two-dollar bill. "I'm thirteen today." I couldn't resist telling her my wonderful news.

"Well, I couldn't care less!" she sneered, instantly shrivelling my soul.

Going to the desk, she glanced in a book, sniffed, took my money and slammed it into a drawer. After locking the drawer she dropped the key down the front of her smock. Then she herded me ahead of her, poking my back with her spiky fingernails.

We passed the ladies with the crossed legs. One was under a drying machine that looked like Mum's preserving kettle turned upside down, and one was getting a marcel wave from another hairdresser.

There were two chairs with sloped backs in front of two sinks on the back wall.

"Sit!" ordered White Smock.

I sat, and she wrapped a towel around my neck so tightly it choked me. When I gagged she gave me a dirty look. Forcing my head back on a tray, she hosed it down with freezing cold water, slopped on some liquid soap and began scrubbing to beat the band with her blood-red claws.

"The soap smells good," I ventured to say.

"It's not soap, it's shampoo!" she corrected, scratching like a wildcat as if to punish me for my stupidity.

I'd never had my hair washed with shampoo before. At home we always melted down Sunlight soap in hot water on the gas stove, then rinsed it out with soft water. Hard water just wouldn't do the job, so Mum kept a pail under the eavestrough spout to catch rainwater. In wintertime all we had to do was melt down some snow.

Next White Smock shoved me under a drying machine. Twirling the dial all the way around, without looking, she left me there to boil.

Meanwhile she went to take care of her lady customer. I couldn't help but notice how much better she treated her than she did me. And I was sure they were talking about me, even though I couldn't hear a thing because of the hot wind blowing in my ears. So I lowered my eyes and stared at the cracked linoleum floor. There were dead curls all around my feet—black and red and brown and blonde ones all mingled together. They gave me the creeps.

I didn't look up again until White Smock yanked me out from under the drying machine, cracking my head on the steel rim. I didn't dare complain.

This time she ordered me to sit on a big leather chair under a weird contraption with dozens of black wires dangling down.

"Do you want nice tight curls?" she demanded.

"I think so," I murmured.

"*What?*"

"*I think so!*"

"Just watch your tongue, Miss Smarty!"

Hurriedly, as if she could hardly wait to get it over with, she began yanking strands of my poker-straight hair through slits in small leather pads. When it was all sticking out, like porcupine quills,

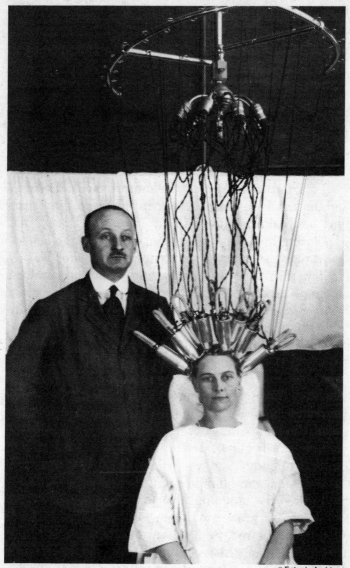

© Eaton's Archives

she took the scissors and began chopping it off in chunks. Next she rolled up what was left, mercilessly tight, onto small metal curlers.

When they were all in place, she lowered the strange contraption close to my head and snapped each curler into a vise-like clamp attached to the dangling wires. Suddenly she moved aside and I saw myself in a mirror on the wall. Just as I realized that I was hopelessly trapped in an electric chair she threw the switch.

I started to shake and the more I shook the tighter the machine seemed to grip my head. So I used my best calm-me-down trick.

Closing my eyes, I imagined myself in the schoolyard playing baseball with the gang. Buster was up to bat and Georgie was yelling from the pitcher's mound, "Okay, all you fielders—moooovvve back! Buster's up to bat!" We fanned out in all directions and Buster made a soaring hit, the like of which had never before been seen. But even with the sun in my eyes I reached up and plucked it out of the air as easy as pie. The roar of applause from my teammates suddenly turned into a loud hissing sound.

My eyes flew open and I couldn't see a thing for the cloud of steam swirling around my head.

"*Help!*" I yelled.

But nobody paid me the slightest mind. Both hairdressers were happily puffing on cigarettes, their backs to me, laughing and joking with their other customers. I knew I was sunk if I had to depend on them to save me. So I closed my eyes and began a fervent prayer. "Listen, God, I know I don't deserve your attention after playing hooky from Sunday School last week and spending my collection on a

Sweet Marie, but I promise never to do it again if you'll just get me out of here."

Then I smelled smoke. My eyes flew open again and there it was, spiralling up from all the metal curlers.

"*Help! Fire! Police!*" I screamed.

White Smock came running, threw the switch and began ripping off the burning curlers, sucking her scorched fingers and swearing a blue streak. My hair was still smouldering when she plunged me, head first, into a sinkful of ice-cold water.

"Everything will be fine—you'll see!" She began rubbing my head in great agitation while the other ladies stood anxiously around us. "I'll give you my very best two-dollar finger wave and I won't charge you an extra cent. You'll be thrilled—you'll see. I've been hairdressing now for going on ten years and I've never had a dissatisfied customer. Isn't that right, ladies?"

They bobbed their heads, obediently, while giving each other furtive looks.

Well, she tried, I'll have to say that for her. But nothing she did could change the fact that my head looked like a ball of wool that a bunch of cats had been fighting over for a week.

"In a couple of month's time it'll be beautiful. Just you wait and see. Mark my words." She gabbled worse than Roy-Roy as she herded me towards the door. "Here, let me help you on with your coat. What a lovely shade of blue. Teal, isn't it? And where's your hat, dear? You don't want to catch your death of cold, do you? Now run along home and tell your mother she's got a lovely daughter and that's the truth."

The old witch. As if her polite words could fool me. And I hadn't brought my toque because I hadn't wanted to mess up my brand-new permanent wave. *Ha!*

Yanking my coat collar up, I retracted my head like a turtle and made a beeline for home. Halfway there I realized I'd forgotten the dratted meat. Moaning aloud, I retraced my steps to the beauty salon, grabbed the package from the window sill, darted old White Smock a final, scathing glare and ran for home again.

I took all the unfamiliar side streets I could think of. But just as I turned onto Veeny Street Georgie rode by on his bike. "Hi, Bea!" he hollered. Normally I would have been thrilled to pieces, but this time I ducked my head down deeper and pretended not to hear.

Then Ada and Ruth called to me from across the street. I pretended not to see them. At last I made it to our back door.

Streaking through the kitchen I threw the meat on the table, ran past my startled mother and bolted lickety-split up the stairs to the trunk in the hallway. Flinging open the lid I rummaged wildly through it, found last year's woollen toque and jammed it onto my head until only my eyes were showing. Then I ran to the bedroom, slammed the door and cried my head off.

At supper time I crept downstairs and slid into my place at the table. *"I'm going to wear this toque for the rest of my life and I want to be buried in it!"* I shrieked.

Nobody laughed. Not even Arthur.

8
Dear Aunt Aggie

Jan. 3, 1936

Dear Aunt Aggie,

How are you? How are Major and Grandpa? We are all fine down here except Willa has the pleurisy and Jakey's got pinworms and Dad's got a gumboil.

I received your most welcome letter some time ago but I haven't had a chance to answer it till now. First, I was busy with my examinations. (In case you have forgotten, I am in the entrance class this year.) I got 72%, which is the best I've ever done in my whole life. Mr. Jackson says he expects me to do even better at Easter. For his sake I'll try, but I don't think I can. (Our class gave him a Parker Fountain Pen for Xmas and he filled it at *my* inkwell! He is so handsome, Aunt Aggie, you wouldn't believe it. Both Gladie and I are in love with him—but don't tell Grandpa I said that!) As usual, Willa got the highest marks in Fifth Form. She will be getting her Senior Matric this year. Can you imagine that? Arthur did well in Second Form and Jakey did good in Senior First.

Did you have a Merry Christmas up there? We did down here, but for a while it looked as if we weren't going to. I'll tell you why. Two weeks before Christmas Dad got a notice in his pay packet saying his wages would be cut from twelve dollars a week to ten. Well, that started a terrible row between Mum and Dad that lasted until Christmas Eve. It was horrendous! (If you don't know what that big word means, Aunt Aggie, because you only went to the one-room schoolhouse in Heckley, then look it up in your dictionary. I use a lot of big words since Mr. Jackson told me I had a flair. I'll put quotations around them so you won't miss any.)

Well, after Dad got the bad news about his pay packet he told Willa and Arthur and me not to expect any presents this year and that made me feel very "lamentable." But on Christmas morning we were in for a big surprise. First Dad made us all shut our eyes and not open them until he said so. Then we heard him grunting as he carried something heavy up the cellar stairs. You'll never guess what it was so I won't keep you in "suspension" any longer. It was a radio! Not a crystal set with earphones like Grandpa has in Muskoka, but a real mantle radio that you plug into the wall. It's shaped like a cathedral. Dad got it for only two dollars from one of his workmates who had been laid off.

So we didn't mind not getting presents after all

because we listened "enraptured" to King George V's Christmas message and to carols all day long. The fires were so low in both the stoves that the house was freezing and the bunch of us were huddled together on the davenport listening to *Scrooge's Christmas* when Mum said "Where's Arthur?" and Jakey said, very seriously, "He went outside to get warm." Then we all screeched laughing. Isn't that a "hilarious" story, Aunt Aggie?

Have you seen Horace Huxtable lately? You said in your letter that you lanced his father's boil, but you didn't mention Horace. Does he ever ask about me? Be back in a jiffy. I have to wipe the dishes.

Jan. 5, 1936

Wasn't that a long jiffy? Please excuse the ink blots but Arthur threw the dishrag at me and it landed on my letter.

Well, let's see, where was I? Oh, yes—for New Year's day we went to Uncle Charlie's. Aunt Ida was there, too, as I guess you know. The first thing she said to me when I pulled off my toque and my hair sprang up like a bush (remember I told you about my hideous frizzy permanent?) was, "Don't you look a fright, Beatrice?" Well, I know I shouldn't say this because she is your sister and all, but she is an "intolerable" person and that's the truth and you know I am not a "prevaricator."

Our New Year's supper was great! The chicken

was done to a turn and Uncle Charlie made four drumsticks out of the one bird and we can't figure out how he did it. For dessert we had plum pudding with money hidden in it. Jakey and Billy and I got a nickel and Willa and Arthur got a dime. Then Billy choked on his nickel and he had to be turned upside down and slapped. So Dad grabbed the money off both him and Jakey and caused a great hullabaloo. I was just going to complain about Willa and Arthur getting more money than me when Uncle Charlie pulled a quarter out of his pudding and stuck it in mine. Arthur turned green but Willa didn't bat an eye.

Anyway, after supper while Willa and Mum were helping Aunt Myrtle with the washing up—Aunt Ida had "conveniently" disappeared—Uncle Charlie said, "Come into the barbershop, Bea, and I'll see what can be done about that mop." Well, he went to work on my hair with his scissors and trimmed all the fuzz off and left me with a headful of soft fair curls. Oh, Aunt Aggie, you wouldn't believe the "transformation." It was almost like a miracle. In fact I think it was a miracle because only the night before I had "entreated" God to do something about my hair. Wait till Georgie Dunn sees me now! He'll hardly recognize me.

After the little kids had been put to bed we played Forfeits—it's my favourite parlour game—and later I won another ten cents for knocking a dime off my nose with my tongue. So altogether I was forty cents richer. Wasn't I lucky?

Well, Aunt Aggie, I must sign off now. Mum is after me to get to bed again. She still worries about me getting lots of rest because of my bronchitis which I don't have anymore thanks to that awful goose grease you made me take. (Gag! Gag!)

I hope you found this letter both interesting and "informational." I tried not to use too many big words but "simplification" is hard for me because of my "potential."

Love and "salutations,"
Your "affectionate" niece,
Beatrice Myrtle Thomson

P.S.: I had to tear open the envelope because I forgot to tell you something "imperative." (Dad gave me heck for wasting an envelope but when I told him I was writing to *his* sister he gave me another one. I guess that's what Mum means when she says that blood's thicker than water.) Anyway, I forgot to tell you the trouble Arthur's in. He and Georgie Dunn (he is sort of my boyfriend but he doesn't know it yet) played hooky from high school and went to the Uptown show at Yonge and Bloor to see Errol Flynn in *Captain Blood*. Well, the next day they wrote each other's notes and forged each other's mother's signatures. Right away their form teacher, Mr. Grumble, got suspicious because Georgie's writing is sort of peculiar. (When he was little he was left-handed and he got slapped and was made to stand in the cloakroom until he turned right-handed.) Mr. Grumble marched them to the principal's office and that night the principal phoned Mr. Dunn and Mr. Dunn came straight over and told Dad. Well, Dad was all for razor-stropping Arthur to within an inch of his life, but Mum jumped between them and screeched, *"Over my dead body!"* So Dad made Arthur stay in for a month after school instead, and Georgie got the same punishment. There . . . wasn't that "sensational" news?

Bye for sure this time,
B.M.T.

About a week later I got a letter back from Aunt Aggie that was so full of big words I could hardly make head or tail of it. I had to look up practically every word in Willa's dictionary. That cured me of my big word habit. At least temporarily.

9
The unidentified hero

I'll never forget the day the king died because we had so much fun.

It was early on the morning of January 21, 1936, and Mum had just tuned the radio in to CFRB. Usually Jim Hunter's news broadcast came on with a blare of trumpets, like the start of a horse race, followed by his hearty greeting, "Good *Monday* morning, everybody!" (Or Tuesday or Wednesday or whatever day it happened to be.) But this particular day he began with a solemn declaration: *The King is dead. Long live the King!* We all gasped and stopped talking and listened to the grim details direct from Buckingham Palace. Then he said that all Canadian schools would be closed for a day of mourning.

Well, we got over the mourning quickly enough because King George V was old and we didn't know him personally anyway.

"Oh, the Saints preserve me!" Mum groaned when she realized the bunch of us would be home for the whole day.

"Yippee!" Jakey flung his primer up into the air. "That means me and Billy can play all day."

"Not until you've cleaned up the mess you made in the cellar yesterday." Mum believed in giving us all jobs to do, even Jakey and Billy, so we wouldn't grow up shiftless. So I had chores to do all morning.

In the afternoon Glad and Ruth and Ada-May and I each managed to cadge fifteen cents and two car tickets to go downtown to the picture show.

On the Bloor streetcar we argued about what to see.

"I want to see Shirley Temple in *Poor Little Rich Girl*," cooed Ruth. "She's so C.K." (C.K. was short for cute kid.)

"Let's go to the Uptown and see *Magnificent Obsession*," suggested Glad.

"Yah!" I agreed. "Robert Taylor is my magnificent obsession."

Ada raised her eyebrows about a foot at that. "I'd rather go to the Tivoli," she said. "George Raft and Ginger Rogers are in a dancing picture there." Ada was nearly fifteen so she was crazy about dancing. "I'll tell you what"—she rummaged through her purse and found a note pad and pencil—"we'll write our names on bits of paper and draw to decide. That seems fair."

We put our slips of paper into Ada's blue felt hat. Ruth squeezed her eyes shut, poked around in the hat and drew out Ada's name. So we headed for the Tivoli.

At Yonge and Bloor streets we stopped off on our transfers at my Aunt Susan's nut store. We saw her in the window heaving a big batch of shiny redskins out of the bubbling oil. "Well, what are you scally-wags doing running the roads?" Aunt Susan joked when we walked in.

She still treated us like children but we put up with it knowing she'd give us some nuts to munch in the show. She gave the other girls peanuts but she gave me cashews. I started nibbling right away. I just couldn't help myself. "Your mother must have been scared by a squirrel when she made you, Bea," Aunt Susan chuckled.

Just then a crowd of people jumped off the Yonge car and followed their noses into the Nuthouse. So we yelled our thank-you's over their heads and made our escape, clutching our hot, greasy bags.

The moving picture was called *In Person* and it was terrific. We discussed it all the way home. Actually we were all dying to learn to dance. Sometimes Arthur and I even tried a few steps when *Shep Fields and his Rippling Rhythm* came on the radio, but we generally ended up fighting because he always blamed me for getting out of step. He thought he was *so* perfect!

That night after supper, since we didn't have any homework, Glad and I went skating at the Grenny. That's what Swanseaites affectionately called the Grenadier Pond.

I didn't own a pair of skates myself so Willa loaned me hers. She still had a touch of pleurisy and couldn't go out in the night air. Arthur couldn't go out either because he was still being punished.

It was an ideal night for skating—crisp and cold,

with bright moonlight and a million stars. Right after New Year's there had been a January thaw and it hadn't snowed since, so the pond was as smooth and clear as a looking glass.

The ice was speckled with skaters, twirling, coasting, some gliding like dancers, arm in arm. (How I would have loved to link arms and skate like that with Georgie!)

Glad and I sat on a log frozen into the edge of the pond, to put on our skates. I had to wear two pairs of Dad's thick work socks with the toes folded over to fill out Willa's skates.

But Glad was even worse off. She had to wear her running shoes inside Buster's skates to make them fit.

Oh, but it was worth it! The sheer joy of sailing like seagulls, arms outstretched, the full length of the pond with the north wind pushing at our backs! But the return trip was another story. With such ill-fitting boots we couldn't really skate at all so we staggered and fell, our ankles twisting painfully as we fought against the wind.

"Let's go to Jasper's shack and get warmed up," I gasped, my words forming little clouds in the air.

"I haven't got any money." Glad was crying now, the tears freezing on her bright red cheeks. "And Jasper won't even let us in unless we buy something."

"I've got fourteen cents left over from New Year's so I'll treat. Ain't I magnanimous?"

"Ain't ain't in the dictionary," Glad managed to laugh as she chipped the tears away with icy mitts.

Jasper's shack, which he'd built himself with

scraps of tin and boards and shingles, was a Grenny tradition. It had clung lopsidedly to the west bank of the pond for as long as I could remember. Its coal-oil lantern winked like a firefly through the bare, black trees. The shack was filled with a peculiar mixture of steamy, pungent odours: sweaty socks, hot cocoa, wood smoke and burning coal oil. Another lantern hanging from the ceiling bathed the room in a warm, orange glow.

"Shut the dern door!" bellowed Jasper as we squeezed ourselves inside. *"You want me to ketch pee-na-moneeya?"* He always said that.

Collapsing on the bench by the wall, Glad and I undid our skates as fast as our frost-bitten fingers would allow. Each person could only stay ten minutes. That was Jasper's rule, because the shack only held twelve people, six on either side.

Wonderful heat radiated out from the makeshift box-stove in the middle. Two rows of bricks were lined up on its flat top and a blackened pot burbled at the back. With calloused fingers sticking out of raggedy gloves, Jasper dropped two hot bricks in front of us on the splintery floor. I paid him two cents each for them.

Gingerly we lowered our sock feet onto the roasting clay. Needles of fire pierced our frozen toes and it was all we could do not to scream out loud. But when the pain subsided, relief came in such a delicious, tingling flood that we *ooohhhed* and *aaahhhed* in ecstasy.

"Anything else, girls?" Jasper was a keen businessman.

"A Sweet Marie and two cups of cocoa, Jasper," I ordered.

Mum said that Jasper never washed the cups between customers and she forbade me to drink the filthy stuff, but I figured what my mother didn't know wouldn't hurt me.

So we each had a steaming mugful and shared the Sweet Marie. That was the end of my New Year's money.

Our ten minutes were up in no time and other skaters were clambering to get in. "Don't get yer shirt in a knot out there!" Jasper hollered through the door. Then he gave Glad and me an extra two minutes on account of the trouble she had lacing up Buster's skates over her running shoes.

Out on the ice once more, warm and refreshed, we headed south again, riding the wind like eagles.

"What's that noise?" Glad yelled to me as she skimmed along on her boots.

A loud *crack,* like summer thunder, split the air. I darted a look over my shoulder and saw the ice breaking up behind us in great gaping wounds. *"Skate faster! Hurry! We gotta stay ahead of the crack!"*

Tilting our arms, like banking birds, we veered towards the bulrushes.

No sooner had we scrambled up the bank to safety than the ice gave way with a piercing *crash* and someone sank, screaming, to his armpits.

"Yi! Yi! Yi!" came the terrified cry.

"Help! Help! Help!" shrieked Gladie and I.

We couldn't make out who it was. All we could

see was a boy's white face bobbing eerily in the moonlight.

People came sailing off the ice from all directions. Inky black water flooded the cracks as far as the eye could see.

Soon a crowd had gathered on the bank. Everyone was panic-stricken, screaming and running and yelling for help, but nobody knew what to do.

Then out of the darkness strode a tall figure in a macintosh coat, his face wrapped up in a woollen muffler. Over his shoulder he carried a long wooden plank. The crowd quickly parted to let him pass.

Dropping the plank with a loud wet *slap* that sounded like a giant beaver's tail hitting the water, he fell to his knees and began crawling carefully forward. The ice cracked as he shoved the board ahead of him.

Now the people had become hushed and still. The only sound was the pitiful wailing of the boy as he clung to the jagged ice.

A minute seemed like an hour. At last, stretched out full-length, the stranger was just able to grasp the boy's hands. Then, inch by treacherous inch, he hauled him in to safety.

Now everyone sprang into action. One man took off his coat and threw it over the victim. Another unbuttoned his windbreaker and wrapped the boy inside. Then he hurried with him in the direction of Jasper's shack.

Meanwhile the man in the macintosh shouldered the plank again and disappeared up the wooded path to Ellis Avenue.

Glad and I, our ankles twisting and turning on the slippery bank, scrambled after the man who was carrying the whimpering boy.

When the door to the shack opened and the lantern light fell on the ghostly white face, we instantly recognized him. Then the door shut and we turned slowly away.

Trembling with excitement, Glad and I shucked off our skates and found our frozen galoshes behind the log. The buckles were solid ice so we left them open and flapped our way home as fast as we could.

I kept my family spellbound as I told them the terrible tale. "And guess who it was that nearly drowned?" I had saved the best part to the last.

"Well, for Pete's sake, who?" snapped Arthur.

"Guess," I tantalized.

"Oh, don't be ridiculous, Bea. Who?" demanded Willa.

In deference to her ill health, I told. "It was Roy-Roy the dumb boy!"

"Ah, the poor lamb," Mum murmured, shaking her head sadly. "Maybe it would have been for the best."

"*Don't say that, Mum!*" I was horrified.

"Well, Bea, you know he's not right. The poor thing's hardly got a thought in his head."

"There's lots of thoughts in Roy-Roy's head, Mum. He just can't get them out, that's all."

She gave me a long, searching look. "Maybe you're right, Booky. Who am I to judge?"

The next day the story was written up in all the papers. Mum had the *Tely* spread out on the kitchen table and we were poring over it together: *Unidentified Man Saves Dumb Boy From Certain Death In Icy Black Waters Of Bottomless Grenadier!*

"You know what, Mum?"

"What, Bea?"

"I think Grampa was the unidentified man."

"What makes you think so? It says here nobody saw his face."

"I know, but I saw the way he walked. You know —big long steps and sort of stooped over."

"Well..." Mum pondered the possibility. "It wouldn't be the first time that Puppa saved somebody from the Grenny."

I decided to go over and ask. I could see it now, tomorrow's headlines in letters two inches high: *William Arthur Cole, Beloved Grandfather Of Beatrice Myrtle Thomson, Admits To Being Unidentified Hero!*

Grampa was sitting by the stove puffing his corncob and reading the paper. There was a macintosh coat hanging on the cellar door.

"You got a new coat, Grampa?"

"About time, isn't it? First one in twenty years."

"Grampa..." I took my own coat off and sat on the stool beside him. "It was you, wasn't it, who saved Roy-Roy?"

"What makes you say that, Be-*a*-trice?"

"Oh, you can't fool me. I recognized the way you walk—and that!" I pointed to the new coat.

"Then I reckon it was me. But I'd be obliged if you kept it to yourself."

"But why, Grampa?" My dreams of being a hero's

79

granddaughter were vanishing like the smoke from his pipe. "You'd be famous. Why, the city might even give you a medal or a citation or something."

Tamping his pipe down with a tobacco-stained thumb he said, "I don't want no medals."

"But gee whiz, why?" I was really disappointed.

"Because the Book says, *Do your good deeds in secret,* that's why."

And *that* was my grampa.

10
A lesson learned

Mum was testing the oven to see if it was right for the popovers. Our new coal-and-gas range (second-hand but new to us) had a heat gauge on the oven door, but Mum said she could still judge better by just sticking her hand in.

While she was stirring the golden-brown gravy with bits of meat floating in it, I set the table.

"Mash the potatoes and turnips together, Willa," Mum said. "That'll be nice for a change."

"Eww, I'm not going to eat any then." Willa screwed up her nose as she started mashing. She hated turnips.

Dad wasn't home yet, so we all sat down without him round the old oilcloth-covered table. I had just poured some more gravy over my second popover when Dad came in the door.

As soon as we saw his hangdog expression we knew something was wrong, and in spite of the cold weather his face was as pale as a soda biscuit.

"I've been laid off!" He blurted out the terrible news as if to get it over with.

All our spoons and forks stopped clinking at once. You could have heard a pin drop.

Then Mum's dark eyes began to smoulder. "There's not a lump of coal in the bin," she muttered.

Dad went all quiet, like the air before a storm.

We finished eating in gloomy silence. Us kids exchanged furtive glances. Even Billy and Jakey, who usually squabbled through supper, were perfectly quiet as they toyed with their food. We all knew what was brewing. Our parents had trouble enough getting along at the best of times—they were so different in nature, like cat and dog, Aunt Ida said. But when they had money worries it seemed to set off fireworks inside them.

Willa washed the dishes and I wiped and Arthur put away without his daily protest that it was girls' work. ("You like to eat, don't you?" was Mum's tart retort to that argument.)

Jakey, who generally took refuge under the table when he felt a fight coming on, went into the front room instead and turned on the radio to hear *Bobby Benson*.

His favourite story had no sooner begun than Dad marched in and snapped it off in his face. "You little fool!" he yelled at Jakey. "Don't you know the radio wastes electricity? And electricity costs money? And I'm laid off! I'm out of work and there's no coal in the bin and you sit there listening to a foolish story. All you think about's your own self. Go to bed and get out of my sight!"

Well, it was only six-thirty and the poor little fellow wasn't used to Dad being mean to him, so he burst out crying and ran headlong up the stairs.

After a while Billy, who didn't understand what was happening because he was only three, sidled up to me and whimpered, "I want you, Bea-Bea."

"Take him up to bed, Bea," Willa whispered. I handed the dishcloth to Arthur and he took it without complaint.

The minute the washing-up was done Willa and Arthur threw on their coats and beat it out the door. But I stayed, cowering on the chair by the stove, shaking the way I always do when I'm scared.

"Please don't fight with Dad tonight, Mum," I pleaded.

It was the wrong thing to say. Instead of stopping her, it seemed to set her off. "What am I supposed to do?" she began to rant unreasonably. "Just pretend everything's all right? How are we going to pay the rent? Easter's coming and you children haven't a stitch on your backs. I'm not a magician, you know. I can't make clothes out of the rag bag."

"You could keep your mouth shut!" Dad snarled as he came out of the cellar way. And that was the beginning of their worst fight in ages.

On and on it raged, for hours and hours, and just as I was certain it was going to come to blows—I tensed myself, ready to spring between them—Dad grabbed his greatcoat off the hook and went slamming out the door. The dishes rattled in the cabinet and I heaved a great sigh of relief.

After that they stopped talking to each other altogether. I didn't know which was worse, the lively battle or the deadly truce.

* * *

One day about a week later Glad and Ruth and Ada and I were standing around on Glad's front walk, talking about boys, when I suddenly caught sight of Dad coming from the direction of the dump. Clomping along behind him in her tattered sweaters and numerous skirts, with her old felt spats flapping around her ankles, was Raggie-Rachel. Both of them were toting bushel baskets full of coal with ash-sifters teetering on the top. They were covered in soot from head to toe. I could hardly make out their features under the powdery ash.

I thought I'd die. I wished the sidewalk would open up and swallow me whole. Turning quickly away, I said, "Can we go in your house, Glad, and listen to *Ma Perkins?*" Without a word the three girls lowered their heads and hurried up the walk. I followed, but before I went inside I glanced over my shoulder.

Rachel had gone. But Dad was still standing there staring straight at me. Even at that distance, and in spite of the soot rimming his eyes, I could see the hurt look on his face. I dropped my eyes and went into Glad's house and shut the door.

That night at supper I made up a question to ask, one I was sure would catch my father's interest. "Dad, when you were in France in 1917, did you and Uncle Charlie fight in the same battalion?"

Dad could always be depended upon to talk about the war, but this time there was no answer. His eyes never left his plate.

"Dad . . . " I tried again.

He raised his head slowly and gazed around, his red-rimmed eyes passing me by as if I was invisible.

"Who said that?"

"Bea said it!" Jakey piped up helpfully.

"Bea? Who's Bea? I don't know anybody by that name."

The rest of the family looked at him as if he'd lost his mind. Only I knew what he meant. And the shame I had felt on the street was nothing to the shame I felt at the table.

I moped around all evening, avoiding everybody, wondering what to do. Finally I went upstairs to get ready for bed. It was cold in our room so I undressed hurriedly in the corner behind the stovepipe and put my nightclothes on. Then I steeled myself and went down to the cellar.

Dad was still sifting ashes, carefully picking out the unburnt black coal with cracked, carbon-caked fingers. He had already salvaged two pails and a scuttle-full. Enough to keep both stoves going for a couple more days.

"Dad . . . "

This time he looked right at me and his eyes, behind the powdery lashes, were infinitely sad. "What is it?" he asked gruffly.

"I'm sorry, Dad." I could hardly speak for the lump in my throat.

"All right, Bea. But let this be a lesson to you, and don't ever turn up your nose at honest labour again."

"I won't, Dad."

He went back to his work and I dragged my heavy feet, in my worn-out slippers, up the two flights of stairs to bed.

11
Helping out

Well, things didn't turn out so badly after all. Mum and Dad started speaking again—Mum was too much of a talker to stay quiet for long. And Dad managed to get enough odd jobs to stay off the pogey. That was important to Dad, not having to accept charity. Because winter was nearly over, the stoves could soon be let out and Dad wouldn't have to pick coal from the dump much longer.

Arthur was able to help out some too. He had a paper route and on Saturdays he gave Mum every cent he earned. Then she gave him back twenty-five cents for spending money.

Willa got a job at Kresge's in corselettes. Her friend Minnie Beasley, who lived in the house stuck to ours on the north side, was working full-time at Kresge's in men's drawers, and when she heard about the part-time opening in corselettes she spoke up for Willa.

"If it interferes with your schoolwork you'll have to give it up. Your education comes first," Mum said. "Your father and I wouldn't be in this predicament, you know, if we'd had the chance to finish our schooling. But that's not going to happen to any of my children. You can bet your boots on that!"

"Oh, don't worry, Mum, I'll manage," Willa said. "Just so long as nobody finds out what department I'm in."

Arthur couldn't resist a snicker. "Everybody will see you there," he grinned.

"Well, you better not show your smart-alecky face at my counter," Willa warned.

Even though Arthur was bigger than Willa now, he was still a bit scared of her. Or maybe the fear had turned into respect. I don't know which.

Of the older kids, I was the only one who wasn't helping out and I felt awful about it.

"You can help by taking on some of Willa's jobs around the house," Mum suggested.

"It's not the same. Besides, I abhor housework. I wish I could help with money."

Then one day something happened that made my wish come true.

Aunt Ellie came running across the street and bustling in our door, wiping her doughy hands on her floury apron. "Franny, a woman wants you on the phone. She asked me if I knew where you were living now and I said right across the road, but she wouldn't even give her name."

"My stars, I wonder who it could be?" Mum dropped the broom in the corner and pulled on her sweater. "Bea, you keep an eye on Billy. I'll be back in two shakes."

Well, she was gone for ages and when she came back she was flushed with excitement. "You'll never guess who it was!" She rubbed her hands together gleefully. "My old school chum, Dorothea Moss. She's married to a druggist now and they're parked on Easy Street." Mum went straight to the sideboard and got the photograph album out of the top drawer. "I think there's a snapshot of her and me in here somewhere." She flipped through the dog-eared pages. "Here it is! That picture was taken at a young people's picnic at Hanlan's Point. My, Dorothea was a handsome girl."

Mum looked at the picture for a long moment, memories flitting across her face and sparkling in her eyes. "Oh, my lands! I nearly forgot to tell you what the phone call was all about." Now she looked like the cat that had swallowed the canary.

"What, Mum, what?"

"She wanted to know if I could recommend a girl to help her with her new baby. A girl about thirteen years old."

"Did you say I'm thirteen, Mum? Did you? Did you?"

"Yas, Bea." That's the way she said yes when she was tickled about something. "And she said she's willing to pay two dollars a week for after school and Saturdays. They just moved to the Palisades— my, the homes are lovely over there—so you won't even need a streetcar ticket."

Mum's face went suddenly serious. "Mind you, I told her plump and plain that you couldn't do any hard jobs because you weren't too strong on account of your bronchitis."

"Oh, Mum, I'm strong as a horse. Watch." I flung my arms around her sturdy body and lifted her off the floor before she could stop me.

"Set me down this instant!" she ordered. I did, but I wasn't even breathless.

"Well, just the same, some of those well-to-do women like to take advantage of poor girls and work them to death for a pittance. But I'm sure Dorothea's not like that, and she assured me she only wants you to mind the baby. So I told her how good you've always been with Billy and she said you can start tomorrow."

Dorothea's baby was a beautiful, bright-eyed, bald-headed boy. I was hoping for a girl because, after two little brothers, I was sick of boys.

But he turned out to be a darling baby. His name was Goo-Goo. Of course, that was only a pet name, like Booky. His real name was Gugenheim. Gugenheim Higgenbottom, after his paternal grandfather.

"I would have named him Hubert, after my father," Dorothea confided to me, "but the Higgenbottoms have pots of money and I want him to be rich when he grows up."

Dorothea was very outspoken like that. I liked her a lot and she liked me. And we both loved Goo-Goo.

But I could hardly stand her husband. He was old and pinchy-nosed and stingy. Once I asked her why she married such an old crock—he must have been twice her age—and she answered with a sly wink, "It's better to be an old man's darling than a young man's slave." Boy, I wasn't so sure about that! Anyway, he watched like a hawk when she paid me, and once when she tried to give me an extra quarter he made me give it back.

Everything went along fine for about a month. At the end of each week I'd proudly hand over my money to Mum and she'd give me back twenty-five cents, just like she did Willa and Arthur. Then one Saturday night Dorothea asked me to stay late to mind Goo-Goo so she and Mr. Higgenbottom could go to the Runnymede to see *Broadway Melody of 1935.*

That night I found out just how stingy Mr. Higgenbottom really was because I stayed for supper. Dorothea had cooked three pork chops, with carrots and string beans. He took two chops and she had to share hers with me. Then he watched every bite I put in my mouth. Honestly, he was worse than Grandpa Thomson.

After they left I did the washing-up and put Goo-Goo to bed. He went right to sleep like the good baby he was, so I didn't know what to do next.

In a while I got bored so I decided to have some fun, and the first thing my eyes lit on was the phone. Beside it was a metal telephone directory with the letters of the alphabet sticking out on one side. I touched the *T* experimentally and the lid sprang open, making me jump. *Tom's Smoke Shop, Lyndhurst 6898* was the first number. I dialled the number and a man answered promptly, "Tom's Smoke Shop!"

I cleared my throat and in my best grown-up voice said, "Do you have Prince Albert in the tin?"

"Yes, ma'am, we do," he replied.

"Then let him out—he's suffocating!" I cried,

PRINCE ALBERT

CRIMP CUT

LONG BURNING PIPE AND CIGARETTE TOBACCO

slamming the receiver down and laughing uproariously.

Next I pressed the *L.* On the top of the page was written, *Liggett's Drugstore, Midway 9507.* This time I decided to disguise my voice by pulling my hanky tight over the mouthpiece. A woman answered my ring.

"Uumm—could you tell me if you're on the Bloor car line?" I asked innocently.

"Yes, ma'am, we are." (She fell for it hook, line and sinker.)

"Well, you'd better get off because a streetcar's coming!" This time I collapsed on the floor, rolling with laughter. Then I decided I'd better stop before the telephone company traced my calls and I landed myself in jail.

About nine o'clock I ended up in the kitchen. By that time I was starving from having had such a skimpy supper. I thought I'd just take a peek into their refrigerator. When I opened the door the light popped on, dazzling my eyes. There, spread before me, was a veritable feast: bowls of peaches and greengage plums, tiny pots of ketchup and mustard and relish on a silver tray that you could spin around, ham and milk and butter and syrup and apples, and a cold roast chicken sitting on a platter in clear pink jelly. Lifting it gingerly by the drumsticks, I stripped the dark meat off the back and crammed it into my mouth. Mmmm, it was good. I lowered it carefully back into the jelly so it would look as if it had never been touched.

Behind the chicken, way at the back, was a brown

paper bag. Curious, I pulled it out and opened it up. Inside were at least a dozen huge, ripple-skinned California oranges. Giant oranges, the biggest I'd ever seen.

I hadn't tasted an orange since Christmas and my mouth watered at the wonderful sight. Grabbing one, I dug my fingernails deep into its shiny thick skin. Juice spurted out, hitting me in the eye and dripping off the end of my knobby nose. Curling my long tongue like a trough I caught the delicious stream and let it trickle down my throat.

"Ahhh!" I breathed ecstatically. But one orange only whetted my appetite. So I snatched another and another. Like a greedy vampire I tore them open and sucked and slurped and gobbled and demolished every one.

When I had finished, and was trying not to burp, I stared in dismay at what I had done. Heaped up on the table was a pile of pulp and seeds and orange skins. And at that very moment in walked Dorothea and Mr. Higgenbottom through the kitchen door.

I thought he was going to have apoplexy. His face puffed up and changed colours, from red to blue to purple. *"Why you—you—you gluttonous, conniving, thieving wretch!"* He sprayed saliva all over the place. *"It's plain to see where the likes of you sprang from!"*

Now he turned his wrath on Dorothea. "This is the thanks we get, showing pity on your poverty-stricken friends," he sneered.

Then back to me. *"Get out of my house! Get out of my sight before I lose my temper!"*

Shaking like a leaf, I tried to apologize. "I'm sorry, Mr. Higgenbottom—Dorothea—I'm sorry. I don't know what came over me." I started to cry uncontrollably.

Grabbing me by the shoulder, Dorothea shoved me towards the hall. "Get your coat on quick!" she hissed. Then she hurried me out the door and walked with me to Veeny Street because it was dark outside.

"You silly goose," she scolded. "Now see what you've done. I'm going to have to let you go. And I'll miss you too. And Goo-Goo does love you so. Oh, Bea!"

"Maybe Mr. Higgenbottom will forgive me?" I snivelled hopefully.

"Oh, sure—and maybe there'll be two moons in the sky tomorrow night. Honestly, Bea, you are the limit. But there's no use crying over spilt milk. Slip over and see me and Goo-Goo when old Higgy-Piggy's working. I'll look for you Friday afternoons. Now get home with you."

She wasn't the least bit mad. Just sorry. I could have kicked myself. If only I had been satisfied with the chicken!

When I came in Mum was just finishing up her ironing. Her face sagged with fatigue and there were dark circles under her eyes.

"Where's Dad?" I whispered anxiously.

"He's gone to bed." She took one look at me and knew something was wrong. "What is it? What's the matter?"

So I told her the whole sordid story. She was mad

as hops and gave me a terrible tongue-lashing. "Beatrice Myrtle Thomson. A girl your age. You ought to be ashamed of yourself, taking advantage of Dorothea like that. And what must she think of us? What kind of a home does a girl come from who would gorge herself on a dozen oranges?" My stomach heaved at the word "gorge."

"Why would you steal oranges? Were they at least small oranges?"

"No, huge," I admitted. "But I didn't steal them, Mum, I just ate them."

"I've a good mind to tell your father." Mum wasn't letting up on me any. "And you know what that would mean!"

"Oh, please, Mum!" I could hardly bear the thought of being razor-stropped at my age. "Don't tell him. Dorothea didn't give me any money this week, so that should pay for the oranges."

"That's true enough." Now Mum sounded thankful to find a legitimate excuse for me. "But what *will* I tell him? What if he runs into Mr. Higgenbottom on the street?"

"He won't because Mr. Higgenbottom drives everywhere in his new De Soto. And besides, he never comes near Veeny Street because of the dump. He says all our houses should be levelled to the ground."

"Oh, he does, does he? The old reprobate. I wish he'd say that to me. I'd give him a piece of my mind. Well . . . we'll say Mr. Higgenbottom can't afford you any longer. That ought to make your father happy. He wasn't too pleased about you working for the old skinflint anyway."

"Thank you, Mum." I breathed a sigh of relief.

"Never mind the thank-you's. I'm not condoning what you did, mind. Now get to bed and we'll say no more about it."

I was so uncomfortable from my full stomach and wounded conscience I could hardly sleep all night. So I gave my nose an extra-long massage.

12
A visit to Birchcliff

After I lost my job at Dorothea's and couldn't help out anymore, I got all depressed.

Then, to make matters worse, Dad sold the radio right out from under our noses to get his two dollars back. Us kids all lined up in a mournful row and watched it being lugged out of the house. We felt like a friend had just died. The front room was as dead as a morgue without it. No more *Amos 'n Andy* or *Charlie McCarthy* or *Fibber McGee and Molly*. It was awful.

To add to my misery, instead of doing better on my Easter exams, I did worse. But Mr. Jackson said not to worry, I'd probably pull up in the finals. The finals! Entrance exams! My heart sank at the thought. So instead of enjoying my Easter holidays I went moping around the house worrying and feeling sorry for myself.

Then Glad came over one day and changed all that. "You're wanted on the phone, Bea!" she said.

"Me? Are you sure?" Nobody ever phoned me.

"Well, they didn't ask for the cat," she joked.

So I ran across the road with her, picked up the receiver off the chair where she'd dropped it and cried, "Hello!" into the conical mouthpiece on the wall.

"Hello yourself and see how you like it," came the crazy reply. "Know who this is?"

I said, no, I had no idea.

"It's me, Tootsie Reese. How are ya, Bea?"

I had to think for a minute. Then I remembered. Tootsie was one of the kids I used to know when we lived in Birchcliff. I'd never liked her much. Why would she be phoning me?

"Hi, Tootsie. It's, uh, swell hearing from you. I've missed you." I had, too. You don't have to *like* someone to miss them.

We talked for a while about old times, then she said, "The reason I'm calling is, my mother said I could have a friend stay over one night during the holidays, so I picked you. Wanna come?"

I had never had an overnight invitation outside the family before and I was thrilled. So I said I'd ask my mum and call her right back. A pencil stub hung on a string beside the phone. I wrote her number on the wallpaper among a hundred others, circled it three times so I could find it again and raced home.

"I guess you can go," Mum said, stirring batter in the big mixing bowl. "The change will probably do you good."

"And guess what, Mum!" I'd saved this news till the last. "Tootsie Reese's family have moved into our 'new' house on Cornflower Street."

"Well, I'll be dashed!" Mum declared as she spooned the frothy batter into the graniteware pan. "It'll be like old home week for you, going back there."

I could hardly wait to see the new house again. We still referred to it that way because it had been brand-new when we moved into it. We had hated to leave its sparkling newness after only six months, to come to live in the shabby row-house on Veeny Street.

Willa drew me a map so I wouldn't get lost going to Tootsie's, since it was the first time I'd ever travelled alone in the city. "It takes three streetcars, so don't lose your transfer," she warned. Mum reminded me not to talk to strangers.

"Don't worry, Mum. Gee whiz—I'm thirteen, you know."

It was a nice, sunny, slushy spring day. I loved the trip, gawking out the streetcar window. But by the time I got to Birchcliff two hours later I was glad to hop off the red wooden trolley and start walking down Cornflower Street—straight back into my childhood.

Stopping at the corner of Lilac Street, I looked at the ramshackle house where our Billy had been born. A huge lump welled up in my throat at the memory of that night. Then plain as day I saw myself, a skinny little ghost running lickety-split with my hoop and stick up the street to Audrey's. (Audrey Westover had been my best friend in Birchcliff. I had phoned her once—that's how Tootsie got Aunt Ellie's number—but when she moved to Oshawa we lost touch.)

Heaving a big sigh over my lost childhood, I continued down Cornflower Street.

And there it was, the new house, with its wonderful upstairs veranda and its beautiful bay window. Inside, I could clearly picture the gleaming hardwood floors and the polished oaken banister with its round-topped newel post.

Just then the door flew open and out bounded Tootsie onto the downstairs veranda. "Hi, Bea!" I hardly recognized her. She must have grown five inches in the three years since I'd seen her, and her hair was red now instead of brown. Mrs. Reese came to the door, blowsy and jolly as ever. "Welcome home, Bea," she smiled.

But the moment I stepped over the threshold all my glowing memories of the new house crumbled into dust.

A horrible smell wafted down the hallway. It was all I could do not to hold my nose. My feet stuck to the grime on the once spotless hardwood floors. Rungs were missing from the banister. The round top was broken right off the newel post. And the lovely bay window, which we had been so proud of, was streaked with dirt and covered by a ragged curtain hanging on a sagging string.

"Well, Bea, does it look the same?" asked Mrs. Reese.

"Nearly," I managed to lie.

That night for supper we had beans and bread. Willa would have died if she could have seen the dishes with egg yolk still smeared on them from the last meal.

After supper Tootsie and I went for a walk. As we strolled around Birchcliff, memories, some good and some bad, came flooding over me. I shuddered as we passed Birchcliff School where the teacher had called me a ninny every day for my zeroes in arithmetic. Mr. Jackson would never do that even if I did get zeroes, which I didn't anymore.

We sauntered past the white frame church on Kingston Road where I'd got saved every Sunday. The choir was practising "He walks with me and He talks with me" and their voices, drifting out the window, made me feel saved all over again.

On our way home we passed Audrey's house and I half expected her to come running out the door. But instead a big, tough-looking boy came out, swung his leg over the porch railing and yelled, "Whatcha lookin' at, Stoopid?"

Tootsie hollered back, "Not much, Beanhead!" After a few more insults we sauntered on.

"Boy! You've got more nerve than a canal horse," I said.

"Nah! He's nuts about me," laughed Tootsie, tossing her new red hair. "You got a boyfriend, Bea?"

I thought about Georgie Dunn. But what if I told Tootsie that Georgie was my boyfriend and then she came to visit me in Swansea and I had to prove it?

"Nah!" I shrugged my bony shoulders carelessly. "I'm too busy to bother with boys. My teacher—you should see him, he looks just like Ramon Novarro— well, he says—"

"What's Arthur like now—cute?" she interrupted.

"You might think so," I answered shortly.

We got home just in time to hear the creaking door of *Inner Sanctum* coming on their radio. Then Tootsie's brothers came in from running the roads, as their father put it, and we all sat down at the sticky kitchen table for a game of cards. We had lots of fun. Then we had tea and toast with jam. Their lackadaisical mother didn't seem to care what time we went to bed, so it was nearly midnight before we hit the sack.

Once settled down in the rumpled bed, we talked for hours. Mostly about Tootsie's boyfriends.

It was very interesting. She told me things I wouldn't repeat to a living soul, not even Gladie. I didn't have anything to add, so for once I was the quiet one.

The last thing I remember before dozing off was the funny, sickly-sweet smell of the bedclothes. But the next thing I knew, I woke up with stinging needles of pain all over my body.

"Tootsie! Tootsie!" I shook her awake. "Something's happening!"

"Drat!" she cried, catapulting out of bed. "Get up quick, Bea, and don't touch the light switch!"

Grabbing my hand she yanked me down the dark hall to the smelly bathroom, shut the door and turned on the light. She took the cake of soap from the dish and lathered it up under the tap.

"What are you doing?"

"You'll see."

We crept back to the bedroom, the squishy soap in her hand.

"Now, you stand by the switch," she whispered, "but don't touch it until I say so. Okay?"

"Okay."

She tiptoed to the bed. "*Okay!*" she yelled.

I flipped the switch and she flung the covers back. Furiously she began dabbing all over the bedsheet with the mushy cake of soap. Frenzied bedbugs scurried in every direction in a vain attempt to escape her flying hand. When they had all disappeared she showed me the soap. It was covered with little brown creatures, their backs buried in lather, their legs wiggling frantically.

"Wow! I got a good batch tonight!" she gloated triumphantly as I followed her, goggle-eyed, back to the bathroom. Using the smooth side of the snaggle-toothed family comb she scraped the sodden soap, bugs and all, into the toilet bowl. Then *swooooshhh*, away they went, still fighting for their lives, on their way to Lake Ontario.

"They won't bother us no more tonight," she assured me, and promptly fell asleep. They didn't, but I scratched the rest of the night anyway. And when morning finally came I couldn't for the life of me use that soap or comb, so I ran my fingers through my hair and let it go at that.

When I got home I told Mum all about it and she nearly had a conniption fit. She made me jump right into the bathtub and scrub myself from head to toe. Then she inspected me, inch by inch, and gave my hair a thorough fine-tooth combing. She soaked my clothes in lysol and burned the Eaton's bag I'd carried my nightdress and slippers in.

"It's a sin and a shame," she declared, her tongue tut-tutting a mile a minute. "That lovely house falling into such filthy hands. Well, that puts the kibosh on Tootsie Reese. You can't go there anymore."

"Darn." I wished I hadn't told her. "And I had such a swell time too. Well, would it be okay if I invite Tootsie here? She's dying to see our Arthur again."

"*No!* Bedbugs travel! Can you imagine what your sister would do if she ever found a bug in her bed?"

I could imagine.

13
The invitation

Plop. A letter dropped through the slot in the front door and it wasn't the right time for the postman. Curious, I ran to the hallway and picked it up off the floor. The very neat handwriting on the envelope read *Arthur and Beatrice Thomson*.

Who would write to both of us? I wondered. It must be some kind of joke. I ripped open the envelope and unfolded a single sheet of notepaper. *You are cordially invited to a surprise party for Ada-May Hubbard on the occasion of her fifteenth birthday at 8 p.m. on Saturday, May 9, 1936, at 24 Veeny Street.* That was only a week away.

"*Arthur!*" He was down the cellar helping Dad.

"*What?*"

"Come see what we got!"

He came up with an inquisitive expression on his face. I handed him the note. After reading it he asked, "Are you going?"

"Sure. Are you?"

"Not if you are."

"Well, I couldn't care less!" I had borrowed that terrific phrase from old White Smock. Then I added, for good measure, "So put that in your pipe and smoke it!"

I had never been to a mixed party before, much less one at night, and I was both worried and excited about it. First of all I was worried because I didn't have any money for a present for Ada. Neither did Arthur, who had decided to go after all. (I *knew* he would.)

Mum suggested giving Ada things we'd made in school.

"Like what?" asked Arthur skeptically.

"Like that lovely wooden jewellery box you made in Senior Fourth," Mum said. She hopped up on the little stool that made her tall enough to reach the top of the kitchen cabinet and got the box from way at the back. Stepping down, she blew the dust off. "This blue bird you painted on it is real as life." She traced the picture with her finger. "I'm sure Ada would appreciate it."

"But the manual training teacher only gave me forty-six out of a hundred on that," objected Arthur.

"Well, you're an artist, not a carpenter!" retorted Mum.

That pleased Arthur so much he went ahead and polished up the jewellery box with Hawe's Floor Wax and wrapped it in some coloured paper Willa gave him.

"What'll I do for a present, Mum?" I asked anxiously.

"Why don't you give Ada that nice set of hankies you made in domestic science last year?" she suggested.

"But, Mum, Miss Boyle said my sewing was the worst mess she'd ever seen, and that I'd never make a needlewoman." (That was good news to me, because the last thing I wanted to be was a needlewoman.)

"Oh, for mercy's sake, bring them here." Mum was getting irritated. "I'll fix them up if I have time."

Mum made time. She even embroidered Ada's initials on each handkerchief and they turned out lovely. Then Willa arranged them, like four little fans, in a flat box with *A.M.H* showing in each corner.

Willa hadn't been invited to the party, but she didn't care because she had a boyfriend now, Wesley Armstrong. He had auburn hair and eyes to match. He had taken her out twice already, once to supper and once to Shea's Theatre to see *Annie Oakley*. Gee, it must be swell to be eighteen.

* * *

The night of the party both Arthur and I were in a tizzy getting ready. Arthur had slicked back his hair with brilliantine and Mum was having a fit about it.

"It makes your nice blond waves all straight and brown-looking," she lamented.

"That's what it's supposed to do," Arthur said.

"Can I use your pink nail polish, Willa, to match my new dress?"

"You can if you promise two things," Willa bargained.

"I'll promise anything. Just tell me what."

"First, stop biting your fingernails. They look a sight. And second, stop massaging the end of your nose. Especially in bed. It keeps me awake."

"I promise," I answered without giving a serious thought to how hard it would be to give up my favourite bad habits. Then she lent me her nail file to smooth the ragged edges and showed me how to apply the nail polish, leaving the moons bare.

When we were all ready Mum walked behind us to the front door, straightening Arthur's collar and fussing with the back of my skirt. "Now keep in mind about Mr. Hubbard and don't go getting rambunctious," she warned.

Mr. Hubbard was an invalid who had been bedridden with sleeping sickness for twenty years. Everyone said Mrs. Hubbard was a saint for waiting on him hand and foot all those years, instead of packing him off to the Home for Incurables like lots of women would have done.

The only part of Ada's father I had ever actually seen was his feet. Once I had gone upstairs with her to the bathroom and I got a glimpse of his feet through the open bedroom door. It was a hot day so he had no covers on. I remember thinking that his feet looked like a collection of bleached bones on the desert.

"Ada says it doesn't matter how much noise we make, Mum," I assured her, "because her father can't hear a thing."

"Just the same," Mum insisted, "I expect you to behave yourselves and not carry on like you do at home."

We both promised, then started walking up the street together, staying as far apart as possible.

"What are you eating, Arthur?"

"None of your beeswax, Bea."

"Oh, you're a card! A real card!"

He laughed and poked out his tongue. On it was stuck a tiny black square. "It's Sen-Sen," he explained. "For halitosis."

"What's halitosis?" It sounded like a swell new word.

"Bad breath."

"Have you got bad breath?" I took a quick step backwards.

"No! It's so you *won't* get it, dopey. Here." He gave me one.

I put it in my mouth and spat it right out again. "Ugh! Vile! I'd rather have bad breath."

Just then Glad ran across the road to join us. He gave her a Sen-Sen and she sucked it happily.

Ruth was invited to the party too, but she had conspired with Ada's mother to take Ada to Bloor Street on a mock errand and to bring her back after all the guests had arrived.

When Mrs. Hubbard let us in I knew instantly why Arthur was so anxious about halitosis. Lined up in a row on the couch were three gorgeous girls who looked like they'd just stepped out of Eaton's spring and summer catalogue. "These are some of Ada-May's high-school chums," Mrs. Hubbard said as she introduced us.

Cora was a bleached blonde (I could tell by her black roots), Nadine was what Mum would call a raven-haired beauty and Fanny was a flashy redhead. *I* was green with envy.

"Oh, we already know Arthur Thomson!" gushed the gorgeous Cora. "Come sit with us, Arthur." She patted the seat beside her and they all wriggled over to make room. Then that silly brother of mine grinned and blushed and went and squeezed himself in between them.

Two high-school boys were there too. Alvin Wetmore (Wetmore!) was fat and short and pimplyfaced. And Harry Greenwood was tall, dark and handsome.

"Bea, I'd like you and Glad to keep a sharp lookout at the window," Mrs. Hubbard said. "The minute Ada-May and Ruth come in sight, off go the lights."

Glad and I stationed ourselves behind the curtains, thankful to have somewhere to look. Just then Buster and Georgie and Elmer Finney came up the walk.

I could hardly wait for Georgie to see me. For once I was pretty sure I looked nice. I had rinsed my hair with lemon juice and put it up in pin curls. Then Willa had brushed it out for me and the way she fluffed it up around my face made my nose look almost normal. The pink lipstick and nail polish matched my new dress exactly. Mum had made it with just a remnant she picked up at an Eaton's Opportunity Day sale. Glad said it was absolutely dreamy. And even Arthur had remarked that I didn't look half bad, which was a fantastic compliment coming from him.

When the three boys came in I stepped out from behind the curtain.

"Hi, Bea. You look swell!" said Elmer Finney.

"Yah!" agreed my cousin Buster.

But Georgie didn't even seem to notice me. His sparkly eyes and dimpled smile were riveted, positively riveted, on those three Eaton's Beauty Dolls lined up on the couch. Glad and I exchanged knowing looks and shrank in our homemade Sunday School dresses.

Darn that Georgie! I decided then and there that I never wanted a boyfriend. And I was never, ever, going to get married as long as I lived.

"Here they come!" Luckily Glad had remembered her job at the window.

"Lights out!" called Mrs. Hubbard.

The room was plunged into darkness. And in the sudden quiet I could hear Elmer Finney whistling through his buck-teeth. He had halitosis, too!

The Hubbards' front door opened directly into their front room, so the minute Ada and Ruth stepped inside Mrs. Hubbard flicked the switch and we all yelled "*Surprise!*"

"Oh, my gosh!" Ada grabbed off her hat and fluffed up her nut-brown hair. "Oh, Mother, how could you? If I'da known I'da changed my dress. Ohhh, for Pete's sake!" She went on like that for about five minutes while we all laughed and clapped and jumped around her.

"Are you surprised, Ada?" her mother kept asking. "Are you really surprised? C'mon now, tell the truth."

"Oh, Mother, how can you even ask? Look at me! I'm red as a beet and shakin' like a leaf."

Finally, Mrs. Hubbard was convinced and the party got under way.

"Let's start the kissing games!" crowed rabbit-faced Elmer Finney.

"Yah!" agreed Buster, "Where's the milk bottle?"

Mrs. Hubbard obliged with a milk bottle, then she laughingly retired to the kitchen.

I had heard all about kissing games, but I had never actually participated before. In fact, I had never really been kissed by a boy except when Horace Huxtable pecked me on the cheek. Sometimes, for practice, I'd kiss the bureau mirror. (Once I forgot to wipe the Tangee lips off the glass and Willa got mad as a wet hen.)

We formed a circle—boy, girl, boy, girl—then Buster gave the bottle a fast spin in the centre of the linoleum carpet. I was scared skinny and thrilled to death, both at the same time. The bottle blurred, like a whirling top, then gradually slowed to a breathless stop. Hoots of laughter broke out when one end pointed at me and the other end at Arthur.

"Oh, no, puke!" cried my horrible brother, pulling a face like he'd just sucked on a lemon.

"Ewww!" squealed flashy Fanny. "I'll trade places with you, Bea. A boy can't kiss his own sister."

We traded, and I never saw Arthur act so excited

before. He went red to the roots of his brilliantined hair. Then he jumped up, bounded over and gave Fanny such a long kiss that I'd swear, if I didn't know better, he'd had some practice.

Changing places with Fanny had put me right opposite Georgie Dunn. By this time he had smiled and winked at me twice, so I didn't feel so badly. But for some reason the bottle never stopped its spin to point at us. After about an hour the game ended and we were the only ones who hadn't been kissed. Nobody else seemed to notice, but I sure had.

"Now let's play post office," giggled Cora.

"My favourite!" cried Nadine.

"Mine too!" agreed goofy old Elmer. He was sitting right beside me now and I happened to glance up under the shelf of his big yellow teeth. Ugh! I thought, shifting over. A person could get rabies.

"You go first, Ada; it's your party!" Ruth pushed the reluctant birthday-girl towards the closet under the stairs. "I'll be the postman."

After whispering her message to Ruth, Ada disappeared behind the closet door.

"I've got a letter here—" announced Ruth, staring fixedly at her empty palm, "addressed to Harry Greenwood."

Harry sprang up, and ducking his head, vanished into the cubbyhole. The rest of us held our breath until we heard a loud *smack*. Then we squealed with laughter as Ada emerged, her face flaming, leaving Harry behind.

"What's it like?" I whispered, trying not to sound envious.

"Oh, boy!" she whispered back, whatever that meant.

One by one the boys and girls got letters, but my name still hadn't been called.

Just then Elmer was called to the closet. Before he left he leaned down, his teeth making me want to run away, and said in a stage whisper, "You're next, Bea!"

Oh, no! I couldn't get my first kiss from ugly old Elmer! I had to think fast. I jumped up and ran to the kitchen where Mrs. Hubbard was preparing things to eat. On the table was a plateful of buttered raisin bread that looked so much like Tootsie's soap it made me gag. Averting my eyes I said, "Can I help you, Mrs. Hubbard?"

"Why, that's nice of you, dear. Maybe you'd like to stir the punch." So I stirred the pink punch that smelled like raspberry jelly until I was sure Elmer's turn would be over. Then I sidled back into the front room and sat down quietly on the first empty chair, which happened to be beside Alvin Wetmore. "I'm gonna getcha, Bea!" he chortled, and bounded for the closet.

I had to escape again. "Ada!" I whispered frantically, "I have to go to the toilet!"

"Well, for Pete's sake, go!" She gave me a disgusted look.

I hurried up the stairs. Mr. Hubbard's door was closed this time so I didn't see his feet. I stayed in the bathroom as long as I possibly could.

I had no sooner got settled down again than Nadine declared, "I've got a letter here for Beatrice Thomson."

Well, by now I was so confused that I didn't know who was in the closet. "Who's in there, Glad?" I whispered.

"That's for us to know and you to find out!" she giggled. Then all the kids pushed and pulled and shoved me into the closet. Just before someone slammed the door behind me I realized with a shock that I was face to face with Georgie. Then we were in the pitch dark. The closet smelled of wet mops and dust rags and lemon oil. My heart was hammering so hard I was afraid he'd hear it.

"Hi, Bea."

"Hi, Georgie."

Our noses were only inches apart. I was glad he couldn't see the knob on mine. His breath smelled sweet and fresh. I wished I had sucked a Sen-Sen.

I felt Georgie's arms go around my waist. Then he kissed me, right on the lips. It was a soft, tender kiss with no smacking sound. I knew I would remember it for the rest of my life.

14
High school!

Willa graduated from high school at the top of her class. Her principal, Mr. Bruce, was determined she should go to university. He even came to our house one night to have a conference about it with Mum and Dad.

The little kids were in bed already, so Mum herded us big kids into the kitchen and shut the door so the grownups could have privacy in the front room.

The three of us held our breath and eavesdropped. Willa had her ear glued to the keyhole and Arthur and I knelt down to listen at the crack below the door. We heard the whole conversation as plain as day.

"Willa is my star pupil," Mr. Bruce was saying, "and I feel it's essential that students of her calibre receive higher education."

"What's 'essential' mean, Willa?" I couldn't resist collecting a new word for my vocabulary.

"Shhh! It means important," she whispered.

"I always knew she'd make us proud," Mum's voice was fairly glowing. "She took top honours in her entrance exams and won the gold medal, you know."

"Good grief," sighed Willa.

"Yes, I know, Mrs. Thomson," Mr. Bruce said gently. "And now to the problem at hand. Is there any way you could manage the yearly tuition fee, Mr. Thomson? It's a hundred and fifteen dollars."

"I'd work day and night if I could," Dad said earnestly, "but I've been laid off at Neilson's and I only have odd jobs to depend on. It's all I can do to meet the rent and—"

"The money he brings in wouldn't keep body and soul together," Mum interrupted.

"Ye gods!" muttered Arthur.

"Well . . . I'm willing to contribute fifty dollars out of my own pocket," declared Mr. Bruce. Willa gasped.

"My word," Mum said, "that *is* generous of you, Mr. Bruce. But the other sixty-five dollars might as well be a thousand to us."

"There's just one chance . . . " Dad began.

"What's that?" Mum and Mr. Bruce asked simultaneously.

"The Veterans' Emergency Fund." A trace of pride filtered back into Dad's voice. "It was set up to help families of overseas veterans. I served three years in France, so I ought to qualify."

"Fine! Fine!" We heard Mr. Bruce scrape back his chair and move towards the door. "Well, goodnight to you both. Be sure to let me know when you hear something."

The very next day Dad high-tailed it down to the Department of Veterans' Affairs. We could hardly wait for him to come home with the good news.

"What are you going to be, Willa?" I was awe-struck at my sister's glittering future.

"I'll decide later," she hedged, starting to set the supper table.

"She's going to be a doctor." Mum let go of the potato masher long enough to rub her hands at the exciting prospect.

Jakey was following Willa around the kitchen, his brown eyes sparkling. "If you be a doctor, Willa, I'll let you take my tonsils out on the kitchen table."

"Me too!" agreed Billy happily. They both loved the gory story about Willa and Arthur suffering through that terrible ordeal on the kitchen table.

"They don't take tonsils out at home anymore," Willa explained, filling the teakettle at the sink. "You have to go to the hospital now."

Just then Dad came in the door. We knew as soon as we saw his long face that the news was bad.

"What did they say?" demanded Mum, her eyes already shooting sparks.

"They said they might have considered it if she was a boy," Dad spat the words out angrily, "but they wouldn't lay that kind of money out on a girl. They said girls don't warrant a university educa-tion."

"And what did you say to that?" Mum was fum-ing.

"I said, 'Then how is it my girl got the highest marks in Fifth Form?' Then I lost my temper and shook my fist in the sergeant's face and he had me put out on the street. It took two privates to do it too," he added defiantly.

Bright red spots flamed on Mum's high cheek-bones and her dark eyes flashed furiously. "If I had the money I'd sue!" she raved. "I'd take it to the highest court in the land!"

"Never mind," Willa put in suddenly. "I'll go back and take a business course next year. I'm pretty sure I can do the three-year commercial program in one. I don't want to be a doctor anyway. I hate the sight of blood."

"The commercial course should qualify you for a good job," Dad said, sounding relieved.

"A good job is not a profession." Tears of frustration were running down Mum's face.

"What about Normal School, Willa?" Arthur suggested helpfully.

Willa shook her head. "I don't want to be a teacher. If I can't be a doctor, maybe I can work in a doctor's office."

Mum and Dad were somewhat mollified, but utterly deflated. They didn't argue about it anymore though.

Willa sighed thankfully; she hated fighting. But late that night I thought I heard her crying herself to sleep.

*   *   *

Well, after all that excitement over Willa my last regular day in Senior Fourth didn't seem very significant. Of course, with the finals looming ahead maybe it wouldn't be my last day after all.

Glad and I both came out our front doors at the same time. It was a hot day for the middle of June, and dusty Veeny Street hadn't been oiled for summer yet. The Canada Bread wagon raised the dust as it trundled by, leaving steaming horse-buns in its wake. Mum always made Arthur scoop up the fresh horse-buns in the dustpan for her flower bed. He hated that job and Willa flatly refused to do it.

"Watch your step, Jakey!" I called as he and Florrie and Skippy went yelling and tripping down the road after the wagon to try to hitch a ride on the step at the back.

Canada Bread is full of lead!
The more you eat, the quicker you're dead!

I had to laugh to hear them singing that same old ditty that we used to sing when we were kids. I guess they were all excited because the summer holidays were coming.

Shortly after the second recess Mr. Jackson got up from his desk and said, "Put all your books away, class. No one will be staying in after three-thirty today."

Glad and I were still sharing the same seat at the front of the room under Mr. Jackson's perfect nose. I liked it there because we faced him most of the time, so he hardly ever saw my profile. It had been the happiest school year of my life, thanks to my wonderful teacher, but I still couldn't shake the awful foreboding that my lifelong nightmare was about to come true and I was going to fail.

I gazed at Mr. Jackson, my heart thumping, as he waited patiently for the class to come to order. I noticed a few silver threads in his jet-black hair, and some spidery lines criss-crossing his blue-shadowed cheeks. A melancholy wave washed over me at the very thought that he might someday grow old.

"Ladies and gentlemen," he began, "today I have some good news and some bad news." Sighs and shuffles and nervous giggles rippled across the room. "So I'll start with the good news. I'm very pleased to announce that eighteen of you have passed without trying. And by the same token, I'm sorry to say that twenty-two of you must write final examinations."

My heart sank. In spite of the fact that I had done fairly well all year long, even in arithmetic, I was convinced that I could never pass the finals. I just knew I'd go all to pieces and I wouldn't remember a thing I'd learned.

Mr. Jackson was holding up his hand for silence. Then he began reading the eighteen lucky names in alphabetical order. "Morris Albert Adams—good for you Morris. Margaret Jane Becker—congratulations, Margaret. Gladys Pearl Cole—you did very well, Gladys . . . " He had a kind word for each new graduate.

"Oh, gosh, Glad," I whispered, sick with envy, "you're so lucky."

"You will be too." She grinned at me.

"Don't be so dumb!" I felt like smacking the self-satisfied grin right off her face.

After that everything went strange. I felt light-headed and there was a peculiar ringing in my ears. Mr. Jackson's voice seemed to float away and the room started revolving around me.

"Beatrice Myrtle Thomson!"

"Yes, sir?" I jumped to my feet and the class snorted and snickered at my obvious confusion.

"You've passed without trying, Beatrice. Now be sure to work hard in high school in order to reach your potential."

My legs started wobbling as I collapsed on the seat beside Glad. Mr. Jackson was smiling down at me, his dark eyes sparkling.

I didn't hear a thing after that. When class was dismissed Glad had to lead me by the hand out the door.

Halfway across the schoolyard I stopped in my tracks. "I forgot to tell Mr. Jackson thank you, Glad!"

"No, you didn't, dummy." She was grinning from ear to ear and now I thought her smile was gorgeous. "You must have thanked him a hundred times. And he asked us both to come back and visit him next year. Don't you remember?"

"Are you sure?"

"Sure I'm sure."

"Okay, let's go home. I can hardly wait to tell Mum." We broke into a run and made a mad dash for our houses.

Bursting in the kitchen door, I slammed it so hard the pie on the window sill did a little dance. *"Mum! Mum!"*

"What is it? What's the matter?" Mum came racing up the cellar stairs, clutching a water-wizened hand over her heart. "For mercy's sake, what's wrong?"

"Nothing's wrong, Mum, but guess what?"

"What, for pity's sake!" Breathlessly she leaned against the doorjamb.

"I passed without trying, Mum! I'm in high school now." As I said the words I could hardly believe them. Imagine—high school.

At first Mom just looked shocked. And then she cried, "Oh, Booky!" and rubbed her bleached white hands together. "Why, that almost makes up for Willa not being able to go to university."

"Oh, Mum!" I grabbed her and kissed her and danced her around the room. "That's the nicest thing you've ever said to me."

She stopped short, panting. Then reaching up, for I was taller than her now, she placed a cool, damp hand on both my cheeks.

"Well, I've got something nicer to say, Bea. I'm proud as punch of you today . . . and I might not tell you often enough, but I love you to pieces!"

Tears glistened in her eyes as she flung her arms around me and gave me a big bone-cracker.

"Oh, Mum. I love you too!"

Talk about happy! I could hardly wait to tell Grampa.

15
Good omens

Ruth and Glad and Ada and I spent most of our time down at Sunnyside Beach that summer, cooling off in good old Lake Ontario. The water was exceptionally warm that year because of the heat wave.

And what a heat wave! Torontonians dropped like flies as the temperature soared to a hundred and five degrees. Eggs were fried on the steps of City Hall to prove how hot it was. Black tar boiled up in the cracks of the sidewalks. And Belle Ewart Ice Company dumped thousands of pounds of ice into Sunnyside Bathing Tank to make it cool enough to swim in. (But was Willa ever lucky. Her boyfriend took her to Loew's Theatre to see *San Francisco*. It was air-conditioned and she said it was so cold it made her teeth chatter!)

The nights were the worst. The temperature didn't seem to cool off even after sunset. Every day Mum would draw the green paper shades down to keep the heat out, then at night she'd throw the

Heat Leaves 550 Ontarians Dead, 225 in Toronto

80-Degree Maximum Forecast for Toronto Today, But Some Days Must Elapse Before Rain

CROPS ARE RUINED

Not So Bad

104—	—Windsor
102—	—Chatham
	—Wallaceburg
100—	—Brantford
	—Galt
98—	—Simcoe
97—	—London
96—	—Sarnia
95—	—Hamilton
89—	—Goderich

ONTARIO'S worst heat wave in more than a century, and the most destructive in its history, was on the move southward today after holding the more than 3,000,000 inhabitants of the Province in its torrid grip for a week.

Toll of Nearly 550 Dead.

It left in its wake a toll of nearly 550 dead—approximately half of them in Toronto—and thousands of acres of parched and burning crops and farmlands, some irreparably ruined.

But if relief, temporary at least, from the burning heat of the seven-day period was at hand, long-sought rains had yet to come. Weather officials have withdrawn from their forecasts the possibility of rain. There was not enough moisture in the air, they said, and although it would probably follow the cooler weather, it would not be for some days.

As temperatures dropped in all sections of the Province before a cooling breeze yesterday afternoon, the death toll lessened correspondingly.

Hospitals Get Respite.

Victims of terrific heat were still being recorded, but not in such alarming numbers. Hospital staffs, overworked for a week as prostration cases

poured in, enjoyed a respite that came just in time.

At Hamilton yesterday, Dr. Miles Brown, Assistant Superintendent of Hamilton City Hospital, declared if cooler weather did not come soon it would come too late to benefit either patients or nurses.

Toronto today awaited its coolest day since July 7. The temperature, weather forecasters prophesied, would be about 80 degrees, but after the 90's and 100's registered during the past week, that reading would be welcomed. Water in storage for city use had dropped from a normal average of 83,000,000 gallons to less than 53,-000,000, a decrease of 30,000,000 gallons in the one-week period.

Ice Prices to Rise.

Ice dealers' at Hamilton Beach warned that prices would be likely to advance as much as 50 per cent. today. Rise in price of fruit and vegetables was freely discussed also as from the parched fruit belt of the Niagara Peninsula came stories of fruit baking on the trees.

Essex County arose to the position of prime producer of Ontario's peas, as the crop escaped serious injury and canning factories were working overtime to keep up production. Elsewhere the crop was said to be an almost hopeless failure.

windows wide open in hopes of capturing a cool lake breeze. There were two windows in the boys' room at the front of the house and we'd all kneel down on the floor with our noses denting the mosquito netting, trying to catch a breath of air.

On such hot summer nights the smell from the Swansea Village dump would knock you flat.

"I can't stand it another minute," Willa snapped one night as she got up from the window sill. "That stench is enough to cause malaria."

"You can only get malaria in tropical countries," said Arthur.

"Well, what do you call this, the Arctic?"

As Willa left the room, Arthur said, "Listen to the crickets. There must be a million of them."

"That dump is a regular breeding ground for the filthy vermin. I've got to go down and spread the cricket powder." Mum got up, rubbing her knees, the sweat dripping off her nose like tears. "I don't know which stinks worse, the powder or the crickets."

The strange city crickets were a real problem for those of us who lived near the dump. They were big, smelly, brown creatures, not at all like regular crickets. They came up by droves at night and invaded the nearby houses.

Once in the middle of the night, not being able to get any water from the upstairs tap because of low pressure, I went downstairs for a drink. I didn't turn on the light because I could see plain as day by the moonlight streaming through the open doors and windows. As I padded barefoot across the dining-room floor I heard a strange *crunch, crunch, crunch* underfoot and felt a sensation like walking on walnut shells. Switching on the light I saw that the floor was carpeted with a layer of ugly brown crickets. The sudden brightness brought them leaping and bounding to life. I let out a bloodcurdling scream that woke the whole family and brought them on the run. The bunch of us nearly went crazy trying to murder the horrible creatures before they found the stairs.

The heat wave was finally broken by a huge thunderstorm. All the kids on Veeny Street ran outside in their bathing suits and revelled in the cloudburst. Even Willa was tempted, but she decided against it on account of her old-fashioned bathing suit. (It was the same as mine, faded blue cotton with a button on one shoulder and a red stripe around the bottom of the knee-length skirt.) But the rest of our gang—Arthur and Buster and Elmer and Georgie and Glad and Ruthie and Ada and I, and even Roy-Roy—joined all the little kids, splashing and cavorting in the soft, warm rain, glorying in our last lovely fling of childhood bliss.

Lots of other interesting things happened that summer too. Willa's friend Minnie Beasley was a runner-up in the Miss Toronto Pageant. And our Arthur won the Harry Horne's Contest with his painting of a green parrot perched on the rim of a Sun-Dried Coffee tin. Underneath it he had printed in neat gold letters the Harry Horne radio jingle: *We all love Sun-Dried Coffee... C-O-double F-double E!* His prize was a huge tin of Campfire marshmallows and his prize-winning picture was mounted in a gilt frame, ready to hang.

Mum was just bursting with pride as she climbed on a chair to hang it on the front-room wall in place of Grandpa Thomson's grim portrait.

"Here, Bea." She handed me Grandpa's picture. "Put this in the back of the hall closet and if the old tyrant ever comes to visit we'll switch them around in a hurry."

"I think it's a good omen, Mum," I said, coming back from the closet. "Arthur's winning the contest."

"What do you mean, Bea?" Mum stood admiring the picture. Now she was absolutely convinced that Arthur was destined to be a great artist some day.

"I think it means our luck has changed, and next Billy will win the Canada's Loveliest Child contest." Willa had taken an adorable snapshot of Billy with her Brownie camera and it had come out crystal clear, so she sent it in.

"Oh, pshaw, Bea, there'll be hundreds of entries. He won't have a ghost of a chance."

She was right, of course. The winner was a little girl who looked like Shirley Temple. Since Doctor Allan Roy Dafoe, the Dionne quintuplets' doctor, was one of the judges, I had to accept his expert opinion. But it took me days to get over it.

The very best thing that happened that summer was Dad getting called back to work.

"I guess you were right about good omens, Bea," Mum said when Dad told us the news.

"And I never once had to beg for pogey," Dad

said triumphantly. The odd jobs he had managed to get, plus the help from Arthur and Willa (and me until I got fired), had been enough to tide us over and we didn't owe a single cent to a living soul. Dad was really proud of that.

With his first pay packet he did the most extravagant thing. He bought another radio. This time it was a floor model just like Tootsie Reese's. It wasn't new and it had a few scratches here and there, but Mum said a good rub with lemon-oil would make them disappear like magic.

It was wonderful, almost like a family reunion, to welcome all those familiar voices back into our parlour. Having a radio in the front room, especially a "DeForest Crosley," made it seem more like a parlour. We could hardly wait for Monday night to hear Cecil B. DeMille intone the magic words, *This is Lux Radio Theatre ... coming to you from Holllyyywooood*. And on Sunday nights when Eddie Cantor sang "I love to spend this hour with you" Mum actually had tears in her eyes.

Boy, I thought, life is just a bowl of cherries!

16
My first date

"Mum . . . I've got something to ask. Don't say no 'til I'm finished, okay?"

"Well, that depends." Mum dipped the collar of Arthur's Sunday shirt in boiling starch, then squeezed the excess into a pot with two red fingers. "I can't promise anything until I know what you want."

I took a deep breath and blurted out, "Georgie asked me to go to the show on Saturday."

"Oh, Bea . . . " Now she was starching the cuffs of Willa's white blouse. "You're only thirteen, and that Georgie has turned into a regular young rip. I've never trusted him since he got our Arthur into trouble playing hooky from school."

"Georgie's not really bad, Mum. Mrs. Sundy says he's just mischievous. And she says he's exceedingly good to his mother. And she says any boy who is exceedingly good to his mother can't be all bad."

"Well, I don't know about that." Mum rolled the starched clothes up in a towel and left them to dampen. "He's always getting into exceedingly bad mischief if you ask me. Why, only last week he stole —stole, mind you—two tires off the rag-bone man's wagon. Then not ten minutes later he sold them back to the poor old gaffer for fifteen cents each."

"That wasn't Georgie, Mum. It was Elmer who did that."

"Are you sure? Mrs. Hubbard told me—"

"I'm absolutely, positively sure. Mrs. Sundy says—"

"Mrs. Sundy is *Miss* Sundy, Bea. You ought to know that." Mum picked socks out of the laundry basket and began folding them inside out. "Oh, I guess you can go if you come straight home after."

* * *

On Friday night I did my hair up in pin curls and decided to massage my nose for an extra half-hour.

"Stop rubbing your nose, Bea! You're jiggling the whole bed!" Willa gave me a hard poke in the ribs.

"Well, Zelda said—"

"Oh, Zelda's nuts. She doesn't know what she's talking about."

I'd never heard Willa use such terrible slang before, so I knew she was really mad. And she was probably right too. Zelda was the kind of person who could make you believe anything, just the way she said it. And the plain truth was that I had been massaging my nose faithfully for over a year and the knob hadn't gotten any smaller. Still, I was afraid to stop now just in case this was the crucial time and it would suddenly begin to work.

"Just five more minutes," I said, circling my finger round and round my nearly-numb nose.

"Bea! You promised!" Willa screeched. "And if you don't stop by the time I count three I'm going to push you out and make you sleep on the floor. One . . . two . . . "

I stopped. The fact was, I really *had* forgotten my promise. And besides, I always lost our bed fights because Willa was a lot stronger than me.

*   *   *

The show went in at one-thirty Saturday afternoon, so Georgie and I started walking up Veeny Street about half-past-twelve. We had never been alone before and we suddenly discovered we were both shy. Then, to make matters worse, Jakey and Florrie came running after us hollering "Georgie lo-oves Bea-Bea! Georgie lo-oves Bea-Bea!" I could have wrung their scrawny little necks. But luckily they had to turn back at Hunter's Store because they weren't allowed to go past the corner.

Finally I asked, "What show are we going to, Georgie?"

"To the Runnymede!" he answered, proud as a peacock.

"Oh, boy!" I had never been to the Runnymede Theatre before but Willa said it was fabulous. It had a blue-domed ceiling that looked just like the sky, with clouds and airplanes floating by. When the lights went out, the whole thing was covered with twinkling stars. She said just to look at the ceiling was worth the price of admission.

"What's on?" I asked, to keep the conversation going.

"*A Message to Garcia* starring John Boles," he said.

"Oh, boy!" I repeated. Willa said John Boles was as handsome as anything and could sing like a nightingale.

As we walked along Bloor Street Georgie unexpectedly took my hand. I was thrilled. But when we got to the theatre, instead of stopping at the ticket booth he led me right past it, around the corner and down the side street to the back alley.

"What are we doing here?" I asked apprehensively.

"You'll see!" He answered impishly, and I couldn't help but wonder if Mum was right about him after all.

At the back of the theatre was a big metal door with no handle. Georgie glanced furtively up and down the alleyway. There was no one in sight. So he picked up a stone and knocked on the door, a sharp, metallic *rat-a-tat-tat*. Nothing happened. So he repeated the signal. This time the door creaked open a tiny crack.

"Georgie?" I whispered uneasily.

"*Shhh!*" He pressed his finger to his lips. Just then, through the crack, we heard the roar of applause and the stomping of feet and the wild whistling that meant the lights had gone out and the show had begun.

"Hang on, Bea!"

I hung on for dear life as we burst through the door and went sailing up the aisle. My feet never touched the ground. Suddenly, Georgie yanked me down beside him into the first two empty seats.

The flood of daylight from the exit door had brought two uniformed ushers bolting down the aisle.

"Watch the screen," hissed Georgie.

We stared, transfixed, at the newsreel, *The Eyes and Ears of the World*. My heart was in my mouth.

But the trick didn't work. Seizing us both by the scruffs of our necks, the ushers dragged us to our feet.

"Hey!" Georgie cried indignantly, "What's the matter with you guys? We didn't do anything."

"Yah? Tell it to the manager, bud!" growled the biggest usher as he shoved Georgie, stumbling, up the aisle ahead of him. As for me, my legs were wobbling so badly that the other usher had to literally carry me by the collar.

Hundreds of curious eyes followed our disgraceful exit. Everybody hissed and booed and whistled as we were dragged up the aisle, through the lobby and into the inner sanctum of the manager's office. Standing in front of the great man himself, Georgie still tried to brazen it out. "We were in our seats for fifteen minutes," he lied.

"Tell us another one, bud!" sneered the burly usher.

I was shaking so violently I thought for sure I'd collapse.

The manager, a mean-looking man with no hair and beady eyes, glared first at Georgie, then at me.

"Well, miss," he spoke in a raspy, nasal voice,

"what have you got to say for yourself?"

Trembling and stammering I said I had nothing to say for myself.

"*Nothing! Nothing is it?*" his voice rose to a squeal. "Well, we'll just see about that! *You!*"—he jabbed a commanding finger at the usher still holding me up by the collar—"Go outside and fetch Officer Bently in here."

Georgie drew in a sharp breath. I darted him a quick look and when I saw fear shining in his dark eyes I broke down and sobbed. And the harder I tried not to, the harder I cried.

He put his arm around my shoulder. "It's all right, Bea," he said. Then, in a voice as steady as a rock, he made his confession. "I'm guilty, mister. It was all my fault. She didn't even know what I was up to. If you'll let her go you can do what you like with me."

I gazed at him adoringly through a blur of tears. Never in my whole life had I known such bravery. And for me! I couldn't get over it.

"Very well!" The manager seemed pleased as punch with himself as he waved me towards the door. The usher shoved me through it and the next thing I knew I was out on the street. I leaned on the glass case outside the show, with John Boles' face looking over my shoulder, until my legs stopped shaking. Then I began crossing and re-crossing the four corners of Runnymede and Bloor, never letting the theatre doors out of my sight, except once when a helmeted policeman rode leisurely by on his bicycle. Guiltily I turned away and stared into a shop window.

At last the show let out and I searched every laughing face. But no Georgie. There was only one answer I could think of. They must have taken him to jail through the exit door where all our troubles began. I didn't know what to do so I went home.

"Don't set foot on my clean floor!" Mum yelled the second I showed my nose at the screen door. So I teetered on the doorstep waiting for her to tell me I could come in. Back and forth across the already shiny floor she swung the long-handled polisher, like a giant toothbrush, until I could see my reflection in the sheen. "Wait until I get the papers down," she added breathlessly. She always covered the freshly waxed floor with old newspapers to keep it spotless for Sunday. When the last paper was spread I stepped in gingerly.

"How was the picture show, Bea?" Mum sat down, fanning herself with one hand and holding her heart with the other.

"Oh, swell, Mum. John Boles is my favourite movie star."

"That's funny. I thought Robert Taylor was," she said, leaning down to read something interesting under her feet.

"Not anymore," I called over my shoulder as I made a beeline for the stairs, pretending I was in a hurry to go to the bathroom. Actually I wanted to change my dress before she noticed the torn collar.

That night after supper Arthur signalled me with his eyes to follow him down the cellar. "George said to tell you everything is okay, so you can stop worrying. He got expelled from the Runnymede for

a whole year but the manager finally let him go home and get the money to pay for the tickets."

"But we didn't get a chance to see the movie or the ceiling or anything!" I protested.

"Well, stupid, it's better than going to jail, isn't it?"

I had to agree with him there.

"George said they gave him the third degree about who unlocked the door from the inside too, but he swore up and down that it was unlocked all the time and they finally believed him."

"Who *did* unlock it?" I hadn't even thought of that.

"What you don't know won't hurt me." He grinned, just as impishly as Georgie had. Then he mounted the ladder-like cellar stairs whistling *Send me a letter ... send it by mail ... send it in care of ... the Birmingham jail!*

Boy, that Arthur! If Mum and Dad ever found out, neither one of us would be allowed to see Georgie again.

I was still awake at about ten-thirty when Willa came to bed. "Well, Bea," she said in that friendly voice she used when she was talking to someone she considered her equal. "How was your first date?"

Not only her tone of voice but her question took me by surprise. My first date ... sneaking into the show by the exit door ... getting caught red-handed ... being dragged in disgrace to the manager's office ... Georgie, his arm protectively around me, bravely taking all the blame.

"Memorable!" I sighed romantically. "Absolutely, positively *memorable!*"

17
No answer

"Mum," I said as I came into the kitchen one sunny August morning wearing my pink dotted swiss dress, "I'm sick of Sunday School. It's boring."

"Well, you either have to go to Sunday School or church. Take your pick."

Glad's mother had given her the same ultimatum, so we both picked church and went together. This particular Sunday was communion, which meant it would be an extra-long service.

By the time the elements were being passed around Glad and I were really bored. So we bent down, heads locked, and whispered behind our hands. "Remember when we were little kids and we thought the bread cubes were angel food cake?" I snickered.

"Yah," she giggled. "And remember how disappointed we were when we discovered the wine was only grape juice?"

"*Shhh!*" Willa poked me hard between the shoulder blades with her hymnal. "Act your age, for heaven's sake!"

Her choice of words sent us into silent hysterics. By the time the benediction had been given our sides were splitting with pent-up, lunatic laughter. But once outside on the sun-baked lawn we became perfectly sane again.

People were milling around under the shady old trees, chatting and fanning themselves with their church calendars. Glad started talking to a girl I didn't particulary like, so I sauntered over to where Maude and Billy Sundy were standing.

"Faith and begorra, Bea, where have you been hiding yourself?" Maude's Irish blue eyes twinkled over her rimless spectacles. "You've been as scarce as a leprechaun lately." Maude and Billy were my best grown-up friends. I used to visit them regularly when I was a little kid.

"Oh, I've been awful busy, Mrs. Sundy." I *knew* she was Miss Sundy, but childhood habits die hard.

"Have you been to see your Grampa lately, Beatrice?" Billy's usual pixie smile was replaced by a reproving frown. "I talked to him over the fence last week and he says he misses you."

My heart thumped with guilt. "I'll go over the minute I get home," I promised.

So I hurried home, changed my dress, gulped my sandwich and was on my way out the door when Willa said, "It's your turn to do the dishes, don't forget."

"I'll do them later. I have to go see Grampa now," I called back through the screen.

"You've always got some excuse!" she yelled after me.

She was right too. I was notorious for sneaking out of the dishes. And when I got back from wherever I'd been Willa almost always had them done.

I started to run lickety-split down the yard and through the lane when I remembered I wasn't supposed to do that anymore. Willa said that since I would be going into high school in September I had to learn to act more dignified. Well, Willa was the most dignified person I knew, so I tried to emulate her. (Emulate was my newest word.)

Mum said I couldn't have picked a finer example to emulate. She was exceedingly proud of her first-born. Sometimes I wondered if Willa was her favourite. Then other times I thought it was Arthur, or Jakey, or Billy—or even me. But one thing for sure, I *knew* I was Grampa Cole's favourite. We were kindred spirits, he and I.

Suddenly I was bubbling over with all the things I'd been up to—things he'd be dying to hear. He was the world's best listener and I figured I could even tell him about my date with Georgie. So putting my dignity aside I ran lickety-split the rest of the way.

Hoping Joey wasn't home, I pushed open the door. It was never locked. Nobody in Swansea bothered to lock their doors, even at night. Mum said that's because most of us were cousins and 'lations and it would be an insult to lock out your own kith and kin.

"Grampa?"

No answer.

I stepped inside the kitchen. There was a plate on the table with dried egg on it, and a grey scum floated on the tea in the saucer.

"Grampa?" I stepped up the one high step into the dining room. The house was so quiet I could hear his pocket watch ticking on top of the Victrola.

He was lying on the day bed under the window. His corncob pipe lay on the floor near his hand. I went over, knelt down and picked it up. It was cold, like the tea. Still on my knees, I looked to see if I'd wakened him.

His mouth hung slack, and under the tea-stained moustache I caught a glimpse of his shrunken gums. His eyes were only half closed and the brown irises seemed oddly hazy. And his usually suntanned, weather-beaten skin was strangely smooth and parchment yellow.

I watched him for quite a while, the seconds ticking by, before I realized that his shallow chest, under the checkered shirt, was absolutely still.

"*Grampa!*" Dropping the pipe, I grabbed his hand. It was cold too.

"*What do you want?*"

I leapt to my feet and whirled around, my heart nearly jumping out of my mouth.

There stood Joey, glowering at me from the doorway.

"It's Grampa," I whispered.

He brushed past me and stared down at the still form on the couch. Then with an anguished cry he dropped to his knees and began shaking his father. "*Pa! Pa! Pa!*"

I let out a scream and ran from the house, sobs tearing at my throat, tears coursing down my face.

*   *   *

The day of the funeral I went over to Grampa's in the morning by myself.

Joey sat on the porch steps, the picture of dejection. He didn't look up or speak; he just moved over to let me pass.

Inside, the air was thick with the smell of flowers. The kitchen was all cleaned up. In the dining room and parlour the normal furniture had all been moved and folding chairs were lined up in neat rows, like in a theatre.

Under the parlour window, surrounded by baskets of bright blossoms, the dark, wooden coffin rested on a long bench. The lid was open and I could just glimpse my grandfather's angular profile showing over the white-ruffled edge. My legs began to shake so I clung to the archway between the two rooms for support. Then I took a deep breath and walked straight up to the casket.

Grampa looked really nice in his new black suit. I'd never seen him dressed up like that before. His wiry hair and moustache were neatly trimmed and his gnarled old hands were folded stiffly across his still, still breast.

"You look handsome, Grampa," I said.

I stood for a long time, memorizing his face. Then I said, "Don't forget your promise, Grampa." He had once told me he'd wait for me outside St. Peter's gate, and not go in without me. Holding my breath, I half expected him to answer. But not a whisper escaped the sealed, waxen lips.

It was then that I realized he was truly gone. Once when I was young he had said to me, about death, "The body is just an old overcoat, Be-*a*-trice.

When it's wore out and you've got no more use for it, you shuck it off and leave it behind."

That's what I was looking at now, his shucked-off overcoat. But it was still *his* overcoat. So my fingers touched the coarse grey hair and my lips brushed the cold cement brow and I said goodbye to Grampa.

On my way out I saw his corncob pipe on the kitchen window sill. I picked it up and slipped it into my pocket.

I passed my boy-uncle on the steps. "Be seeing you, Joey."

"Be seeing you, Bea."

I wasn't afraid of him anymore.

I don't remember much about the funeral, except for one incident. Just before the service was about to begin—every chair was filled and the men were standing all along the walls—who should arrive but Raggie-Rachel.

She came in through the kitchen door and the men sucked in their stomachs to let her pass. The undertakers were just about to close the lid when they saw her coming towards them and stepped back hastily. A hush fell over the assembly. She was wearing her usual summer rig and she looked for all the world like a bundle of rags. But out of respect she had pulled on a frayed black sweater, the buttons done up all askew, over her raggy dresses.

Mum and my aunts stirred nervously, not knowing what to expect. I was in the second row so I got up, squeezed past Willa and went and stood beside Rachel.

"Hello, Rachel." I didn't know what else to say.

She didn't answer me directly. But her voice, when she spoke, was calm and natural. "He was a good man, Mr. Cole. He saved my boy. We'll never see his like again." She reached into the coffin and patted his parchment hands. Then she turned and let herself out the front way. The grey wreath on the door rustled softly as she closed it behind her.

I only wished he could have heard her words. He would have liked them a lot better than what the preacher said.

18
Come!

After the funeral I went all melancholy. Mum didn't know what to do with me.

"If only I had gone over last week, Mum," I reproached myself bitterly, remembering Mr. Sundy's words. "Maybe he felt sick and nobody knew."

"I don't think so, Bea. He was over here borrowing flour for potato cakes on Wednesday and he seemed fit as a fiddle then."

"Did he ask for me?"

"Yas, and I said you were down at Sunnyside swimming with your friends. And he said—"

"What, Mum, what?"

"Well . . . " She set the iron on end, wet her finger on her tongue and tested the iron to see if it was hot enough. "He said he missed you, but he was glad you were having a good summer. Not like last year when you were so sickly."

"I hate myself!" I exploded vehemently.

"Ah, you mustn't fret yourself like that, Booky. Everybody has regrets. I sure had plenty when

147

Mumma went home." She shook her head sadly at the memory, folded the smooth dishtowel and spread out a wrinkled one on the board. "You've got nothing to flay yourself for. You were good to Puppa. Many's the time I heard him say he wouldn't have known what to do without you." That made me feel even worse.

A week went by and I still couldn't shake the sadness. Willa bought me a new lipstick to cheer me up since mine was nearly gone and I had to dig it out with a hairpin. Arthur even offered to take me to see *Rin Tin Tin*.

"Want me to read you a story, Bea?" asked Jakey. He was a good reader now, and knew his First Book off by heart.

"Maybe after, Jakey," I replied listlessly.

"Bea-Bea." Billy's big blue eyes searched my face anxiously. "Don't you love me no more?"

"Sure I do, Billy." I hauled him up on my lap and gave him a big bear-hug. He had grown so much that his toes were touching the floor. "What makes you say such a silly thing?"

"You don't play with me no more," he said plaintively.

"I'm sorry, Billy," I sighed, blowing a furrow through his fine, fair hair. It seemed as if I'd been neglecting everybody I loved that summer. "I'll play with you soon, I promise."

"Run along and leave Bea alone, Billy," Mum said. Then she took the ironing board down from between the two chairs and hid it behind the dining-room door. "Maybe tomorrow we'll take a run down to Eaton's and get you some new shoes for high school, Bea. What do you say to that?"

Ordinarily the prospect would have tickled me pink. But today I just said okay because I knew that's what she wanted to hear. Then the next day I worked myself up to a bilious attack and I stayed in bed all day.

On the following Saturday Mum came home all played out from helping her sisters tidy up Grampa's things. Handing me a musty old shoebox she said, "Here's a job for you, Bea. Sort through that box and see what on earth's in it. You might find something you'd like to keep."

It was mostly rubbish in the box. Old receipts and yellowed newspaper clippings and broken spectacles and bits of stale tobacco. Then I found a tea-stained envelope with my own handwriting on it. It was the letter I had sent Grampa from Muskoka the summer before.

"He didn't answer it, Mum."

"No. Puppa wasn't much of a writer. But he sure was pleased as punch to get it. He told me every word you said." She reached out and stayed my hand as I was about to open it. "Don't read it now, Bea. Put it away with your keepsakes."

I had just about given up finding anything else worthwhile when, at the bottom of the box under all the junk, wrapped carefully in layers and layers of tissue paper, I found a perfectly preserved tintype of a woman and a boy.

The woman in the photograph sat in a wicker chair. She wore a long black dress with a high, ruffled collar. Her dark hair was parted in the middle and drawn back severely into a tight bun, but on either side a few strands had come loose and curled towards her large dark eyes. Mum's hair did that sometimes when she tried to tuck it up under her dustcap. One or two curls always managed to pop out onto her temples.

The boy stood beside her, his hands crossed dutifully on her lap. He wore an old-fashioned velvet suit and a big bow tie. He had thick black hair and solemn dark eyes. I recognized those eyes instantly.

Mum was looking over my shoulder. "It's Grampa, isn't it, Mum?"

"Yas." She took the picture gently into her hands. "My, he was a handsome lad. And that's his mother, my Grandma Cole. Only she was an Arthur before she married Matthew Cole. That's where our Arthur gets his name." She studied the picture a moment longer. "I don't remember either one of my grandparents, more's the pity, but Puppa said he lifted me up to see both of them in their coffins."

"Oh, Mum, that's awful!"

"Yas. I think so too. That's why I didn't take Jakey or Billy over. But that's what folks did in those days. Everyone was obliged to pay their last respects regardless of their age."

She handed me back the picture. I looked long and hard at Grampa—a little boy, just like Jakey. A pain throbbed in my throat. Then I switched my gaze to his mother. She was dark like Grampa and Mum and Jakey, but...

"*Mum!* Do you know what? Your grandmother's got my nose!"

Mum came over and scrutinized the picture again. "Well, by Jove, you're right, Bea. Doesn't that beat all! Only it's the other way around: you've got her nose. So I guess that proves you do belong to me after all. And here I always thought you were one-hundred-percent Thomson." She laughed and gave my new-found nose a pinch that made it stick together. She was always *doing* that!

"I wish I'd got her eyes instead of her nose," I grumbled, wriggling that offensive part of me, like a rabbit, to make it come unstuck.

"Well, I wouldn't complain if I were you." She sounded a bit miffed. "I'll have you know my grandmother was considered something of a beauty in her day."

"Really?" I jumped up to peer in the mirror hanging over the sink, in hopes that a minor miracle had taken place in the last few seconds. Turning sideways, I swivelled my eyes around to get a view of my profile. "It still looks too big to me," I said glumly.

"Well, that's because you haven't quite grown into it yet. But mark my words, Bea, you're getting better-looking every day."

At last I allowed myself to be convinced. "Then maybe I won't need to rub it anymore." I sighed with relief at the thought of being rid of that tiresome nightly ritual.

"Well, thank goodness for small blessings," remarked Willa drily as she swept the floor with the cornbroom.

Carefully I rewrapped the tintype and took it and my letter upstairs to store among my keepsakes in an old chocolate box. My keepsakes were a strange assortment: the little china horse, Reddy's bronze feathers (all that was left of my poor little chicken), my horsehair bracelet that I didn't wear anymore but kept in memory of Major (who was still alive, thank goodness), the corncob pipe, a dried rose from the family wreath and the ribbon with *Puppa* written on it. (There was no *Grampa* ribbon or I would have saved it too.) Putting my letter and the tintype flat on the bottom of the box under the other stuff, I replaced the lid. On the lid I had pasted a white piece of paper over Laura Secord's picture, and on it I had printed in big letters: *MEMORIALS OF MY CHILDHOOD. THIS BOX BELONGS TO BEATRICE MYRTLE THOMSON. ALL OTHER INDIVIDUALS KEEP OUT!*

After shoving the box to the back of my bureau drawer I went straggling downstairs again. The pungent odour of the pipe and the sweet fragrance of the rose had brought back, in full force, my melancholy mood.

Mum was stirring a big pot of hamburger stew on the stove. Normally that lovely smell would have made me ravenous, but today it just made me feel queasy.

"Mum."

"Yas, Booky."

"When I was a child, Grampa promised me once that instead of going straight into heaven he'd wait outside the gate for me. Do you believe that?"

Her back was to me and she stood stock still for a moment. Her hands became busy dropping soft blobs of dough into the bubbling brown liquid. Then she covered the pot with an inverted plate. When she turned around her eyes were dark pools of tears. "Well," she answered huskily, "Puppa had a reputation for always being as good as his word."

That night at supper I couldn't swallow my stew.

"Eat up," Dad said automatically.

"I can't." I pushed my plate away.

"What's that old saying carved on our breadboard?" he asked meaningfully.

I'd cut up so much bread on that board I knew the words off by heart. But Jakey beat me to it. "It says 'Waste Not, Want Not'!" he piped up proudly.

"That's right," agreed Dad. "Now eat up, Bea."

"I'm sorry, Dad, but I've got a sick headache." I started rubbing my brow to prove it.

"Bea"—Dad broke into a fluffy dumpling and the steam escaped with a little puff—"why don't you drop your Aunt Aggie a line?"

What a nice thing to hear when I was expecting a lecture! "Gee, thanks, Dad. I think I will." Then, trying to please him, I ate a snowy white dumpling even though it did upset my stomach.

After supper Willa wordlessly took my place at the sink. Dad brought me the bottle of ink and a writing tablet. Mum got the pen out of the sideboard drawer. "Oh, pshaw, the nib's broken," she said. "Half the point's missing."

"I know where there's a new one." Arthur ran upstairs and got it, licked the oil off, pulled out the broken piece and inserted the new one ready to use.

Everybody was so nice to me I couldn't get over it. And I felt a little better just writing Aunt Aggie's name at the top of my letter.

Dear Aunt Aggie,

I guess you know by now that my Grampa Cole is dead. Dad says that you and Grandpa Thomson are alone on the farm this year because Uncle Wilbur asked Aunt Ida to come back and live with him. (Aunt Ida says he *begged* her to come home. I find that hard to swallow.) Anyway, what I'm writing for is to ask you if I can come up and spend the rest of the summer with you. I really need to talk to you, Aunt Aggie. Tell Grandpa Thomson that I won't be any trouble this year because I am all grown up now. I am not a child anymore.

> Please answer immediately,
> Your loving niece,
> Beatrice

Three days later Aunt Aggie's reply slipped through the slot in our front door. The envelope was so thin I thought she had forgotten to put her letter in. Usually her letters were just bursting at the seams with all the Muskoka news.

Anxiously I tore it open. Out onto the dining-room table dropped a single sheet of paper with one huge word scrawled on it in letters two inches high: *COME!* And pinned to the corner of the page was a round-trip train ticket to Huntsville. All bought and paid for. Imagine!

* * *

The night before I left the whole gang came over to say goodbye. It was almost like a going-away party except nobody had been invited. Even Roy-Roy had come over earlier in the day—I don't know how he got wind of my trip—and brought me a catfish he'd caught by hand. I promised him I'd have it for my last supper. Of course, the minute his back was turned Mum wrapped it up in a pile of newspapers and threw it straight into the garbage. Willa said we'd be lucky if we ever got the smell out of the house. But Mum said it was the thought that counted.

Glad gave me a Sweet Marie to eat on the train. "Try to cheer up, Bea," she whispered worriedly. I said I'd try. Ruth gave me a brand-new *Silver Screen* with Myrna Loy and William Powell on the cover. And Ada loaned me her latest Elsie Dinsmore book. Arthur gave me a nickel and Willa gave me a dime and Dad had already given me a shinplaster to spend in Huntsville.

Georgie was the last to leave. When we were alone in the hallway he reached inside his shirt and pulled out a flat package wrapped in white paper and tied with a pink ribbon. All this time it had been next to his skin so it was kind of sweaty because it was a hot night. But I didn't mind.

"Promise you won't open it until you're on your way?" he said. I promised. He bent down—he was a lot taller than me now—and kissed me right on the mouth. Then he high-tailed it out the door before either one of us had a chance to be embarrassed.

Mum went with me the next morning to Union

Station. I was wearing a new blue dress with a white bolero. It wasn't that the pink dotted swiss was worn out or anything—I had actually outgrown it! Even when Mum let the seams out it didn't fit me properly, so there was nothing to do but make me a new one.

Union Station was right across Front Street from the Royal York Hotel. "The Royal York looks something like a castle, doesn't it, Mum?"

"And so it should," Mum said, "because that's where the Prince of Wales stayed on his visit to Toronto." I stared up at all the hundreds of windows, trying to figure out which one the royal eyes had actually looked out of.

I had never been inside Union Station before so I was absolutely enthralled by its cathedral ceiling and stone archways and marvellous marble floors. We sat on a hardwood bench under the clock, waiting for our train to be announced. I got a crick in my neck gazing up at the high, curved dome and reading all the names of the provinces carved around the edge.

"Now, here's your lunch." Mum sounded kind of agitated. "All your favourite foods are in it. Bologna sandwiches on white bread with store-bought mustard, and a little jar of your Aunt Ellie's rhubarb preserves. I've put a kitchen spoon in to eat it with, so don't lose it or I'll be one short. Your Aunt Susan sent you this box of nuts. And here's two big oranges from Dorothea. Now I want you to eat up every crumb because you've been looking awful pasty-faced since Puppa went home."

I winced and she hurried on. "Oh, mercy, I'm sorry for reminding you, Bea. But that's life, isn't it?" Then she gave me a big, long bone-cracker as if to try to make amends for life.

At last we heard the echoing voice of the train announcer floating through the vast hall, telling us where the train was leaving from.

Mum persuaded the trainman to let her go with me to the tracks by telling him that I'd never travelled alone before and that I was only thirteen years old. "Thirteen and a half—geeez!" I muttered indignantly. He smiled and let us both go down the stairway.

The train was half empty so I found a window seat easily and stuffed my grip under it. Then I looked for Mum out the streaky glass. I saw her before she saw me. She was searching all the windows, her forehead furrowed in a frown. Suddenly, from this strange perspective, she looked different to me—smaller and sadder and just a little bit old. The sight of her pierced my heart. "Don't die, Mum!" I cried instinctively. I don't know whether I spoke out loud or not.

The train began to move and she hadn't seen me yet. I banged on the window, frantically, and our eyes met. Then her whole countenance changed and she burst into a radiant smile. We waved and waved until we lost each other from sight.

I settled back on the seat and gazed out the window.

The train wended its way through the city, tooting at crossings and spewing black smoke in its wake. Women in their back yards, their mouths full of clothes pins, stopped just long enough to give the sooty monster dirty looks.

Then came the countryside, meadows and barns and horses and cows and red-winged blackbirds on fenceposts. And I was on my way.

That's when I remembered Georgie's present.

My fingers trembled as I undid the bow and tore off the sweat-stained paper. Inside was the most beautiful box of stationery I had ever seen. It was pale blue with a tiny forget-me-not in the corner of each page. A folded sheet of ordinary paper lay on top. I opened it and read:

From your most ardent admirer.
Guess who! Give up? I'll give you a hint. His initials are G.D.
Write soon. XXXOOO

It was my very first love note. I planned to answer it the minute I arrived.

Sighing blissfully, I gazed dreamily out the window. The train began steaming up a hill. Out of the morning mist it rose, into the dazzling sunlight.

And with it rose my spirits.

Bernice Thurman Hunter

There are three books in Bernice Thurman Hunter's popular *Booky* trilogy. *That Scatterbrain Booky* was the winner of the 1981 IODE Award and runner-up in the Toronto Book Awards. *With Love from Booky* and *As Ever, Booky* completed the series.

Now Bernice is creating another trilogy with an equally appealing heroine. *A Place for Margaret* was published in 1984 and *Margaret in the Middle* is due to be published in 1986. Bernice is currently writing a third *Margaret* book in the series.

Bernice also enjoys meeting her readers and visiting schools and libraries all over Ontario.